UNBRIDLED TRAILS

Book #3
Montana Trails series
Clearwater County Collection
Bonnie R. Paulson

ISBN-13: 978-1943377107

DEDICATION

To Bear – I love you.

To Melissa Scherr – your knowledge about the insect world and love for the creepy crawlies helped so much in developing Sherri into such an interesting character. Thank you!

To Lysette – thank you so much for the great title!

Team Paulson! You're the best!

And Mandie… No words.

Jill and Brooklyn, thank you for the amazing critiques. I owe you!

Captiva Publishing, LLC

Bonnie R. Paulson

www.bonnierpaulson.net

Copyright © 2016 Bonnie R. Paulson

Family Tree or Grouping
Montana Trails

Rourke:

Nathan	Broken Trails, Book 1 with Emma
	Untamed Trails, Book 10 with Lily
Stefanie	Hidden Trails, Book 4 with Drake
Hannah	Lost Trails, Book 9 with Zander

Darby:

Jareth	Forbidden Trails, Book 2 with Cyan
Kyle	Unbridled Trails, Book 3 with Sherri
Ruby	Forsaken Trails, Book 7 with Sloan

Johnson:

Ryland	Endless Trails, Book 6 with Amy
Damon	Forgotten Trails, Book 5 with Rachiah

Two-Claw:

(not family, close friends)

Rachiah	Forgotten Trails, Book 5 with Damon
Maverick	Lonesome Trails, Book 8 with Morgan

Unbridled Trails

A vengeful cowboy seeking justice loses his heart to a damsel-in-distress, but can the results of saving her outweigh their chance at love?

Kyle Darby doesn't want to be a lonely ranch hand forever. If he can help his cousin run a ranch, his chances at future foreman will be drastically increased. But his need to find revenge for his sister clouds his logic.

Sherry isn't into dating or anything normal - she studies bugs for crying out loud. When Kyle rescues her one night at a bar, she finds it hard to believe his continued interest is sincere. Used to saving herself and her heart, Sherry has to accept that sometimes she needs help.

With her life hanging in the balance, Sherry has to learn to rely on someone else - Kyle.

Can she do it without losing her heart? Or are they both destined to just be along for the ride?

Chapter 1

Summer 2002

Sherri

Insects expected so much less than humans.

"Rachiah, I'll try to make it down, but no promises, okay?" Sherri leaned toward the phone base secured to the ornate side-table Cyan's mother had picked out at a farmer's market. "I gotta get going, though. Cyan is taking me to Billings. Gotta get there tonight." She hadn't purchased her own car yet. First thing on her list since she'd secured a solid job.

They hung up, Sherri more irritated than before. Why did Rachiah think Sherri was at everyone's beck and call? Especially hers?

Thrusting her hands on her hips, Sherri stormed into the foyer where Cyan stacked their bags. "Look, I'm fine with Rachiah heading to Wyoming to find her dad. I get that. But why do *you* have to stay *here*? Come with me. We can go visit 'Chiah on long weekends." Sherri's last-ditch attempt to make an old argument sound fresh missed its mark. And she knew it.

Everything paled for Cyan compared to the chance to see Jareth more. Heck, Sherri couldn't even offer the prospect of hot entomologists because *one*, Cyan wouldn't care, and *two*, Cyan wouldn't believe her.

Sherri didn't blame her. Most entomologists weren't exactly approached for modeling jobs.

Sighing, Cyan straightened and pushed her blue-streaked dark hair to the side. "You're the one who has to work for the forest service in Billings – chasing those cow maggots." She grinned and wrinkled her nose.

"Beetles." Sherri grinned, hefting her tarantula cage with Tommy inside into her arms with extreme care. She'd have to get him a traveling case. He would love their trip. Hopefully. If she was lucky, she'd be able to find some crickets and grasshoppers. She only fed him bugs. Some tarantula owners fed their arachnids mice, birds, and small lizards. Sherri couldn't do that.

"I'm just glad to be free from your spider for a bit." Cyan shook her head. "I love you, Tommy, but a girl needs her space." She shuddered and shifted to lean her hip against the chair behind her.

Sherri sighed, jutting her jaw to the side. "How many times do I have to tell you? Tarantulas aren't spiders. They're *false spiders*. The biggest teller is that their fangs point down. True spiders have fangs that point horizontally."

"Right, I think I remembered that." Cyan winked, tapping her fingertips on the counter and laughing. "I don't think the bugs are fun, at all. Spiders or not." She waved her hand, pursing her lips into a semblance of a scowl. "They're all gross." She faked gagging.

But bugs weren't gross and Sherri didn't feel like explaining once again how important studying the migration pattern of the invertebrate population in the Billings area was. Cyan only cared about the wolves or anything else endangered. What Cyan didn't seem to understand was that without the insects, there wouldn't be any species to protect.

Cyan sobered and bit her lip. She shuffled her feet. "I wish it wasn't so far away."

"I know." Sherri refused to give in to the melancholy of leaving her second childhood home with its comforting aromas of burning herbs and easy access to essential oils and all things vegan. Not to mention the easygoing attitude of Mr. and Mrs. Burns toward Sherri's multi-legged pets. They never freaked out over a misplaced tarantula or a curious rhinoceros beetle crawling around the kitchen. She didn't want to leave.

But at the same time, she needed to get out on her own. She needed to do something, anything, on her own.

"Promise you'll be back." Cyan pierced Sherri with a glare. "That can't be your forever home." She would hold Sherri to her promise, even if it was made under duress.

The promise wasn't a difficult one to make. "Of course. You're my family." Sherri reached for Cyan with her empty arm, embracing the girl she'd do anything for. As much as Sherri loved her real family, there was something to be said for her girls, who would do anything for her – even live with her bugs.

Billings wouldn't hold her there forever.

She'd be back.

She just didn't know when.

~~~

Rachiah

"When was the last time you just did something because you had to and not because you wanted to?" Rachiah shook her head, smirking at her reflection in the mirror. "Wait, that's not right.

Except it was right. She wasn't going to Wyoming because she wanted to. She could feel deep down in her gut that she needed to be there, looking for her dad. Why would anyone want to stop her from doing that?

She picked up her phone sitting on the bathroom counter and dialed Cyan. After the first ring, Cyan picked up, her *hello* bright and welcoming.

Rachiah took a deep breath, her amusement suddenly fading to sadness. "Do you think she'll forget us?" The question was ridiculous, but she couldn't help worrying about Sherri. Cyan had gone off and fallen in love. Why wouldn't Sherri? And if she fell for someone down in Billings, she'd never be home to see her friends who needed her more than they could tell her.

Cyan's volume dropped and she, too, took on a more serious tone. "She won't forget us. She'll be back. Even if I have to let loose some bugs to bring her home."

"Yeah, okay. I'll hold you to that." Rachiah sighed and moved toward the door of the bathroom. "I'll see you when I get back. Don't kiss Jareth so much he forgets to breathe." She laughed as they hung up, biting back her jealousy that she had to go look for someone she shouldn't have to and dream of something she had no time for.

Love wasn't meant for everyone apparently.

Sherri

2003

Midsummer

Nothing was more appealing than the scent of dirt after a much-needed refreshing rain.

Sherri knelt, one knee resting on the damp mosses on the forest floor outside of Billings, Montana. The summer had taken its toll, the crust of the ground dry even under newly dampened needles.

Dark specks littered the green underbellies of leaves on the lower brush.

Somehow Sherri always spotted the telltale signs of the insects she sought. She'd much rather crawl around in the dirt of the forest floor than sit at a desk or talk to people. Reports of her findings were as close as she got to office work. Her idea of the perfect job always came back to animals. Talking to people wasn't her favorite thing.

Just thinking of the latter sent a shudder through her. A job offer to teach and research at the university hadn't been big enough to overrule Sherri's desire to stay away from the idiot students. She'd graduated and hadn't returned for her doctorate for a reason.

She snapped some pictures of her findings and recorded information in a small notebook she carried in a pocket of her shirt. She wasn't there to interrupt the habitat, just observe. Just watching her surroundings was closer to her idea of heaven than anything else.

The radio clipped to her waist crackled. "Sherri, you 'bout done? Over."

What time was it? Had she really been out there all day? Yanking the radio toward her lips, Sherri searched the surrounding woods. She pushed the button as late afternoon sunlight shafted through the sparse branches. "Copy. I'm coming in. Over."

Man, she was going to miss that place. Her last radio call with the Billings Park and Recreation didn't satisfy her need for connection. No one there had. They didn't need her expertise on Western Pine Beetles anymore. The drought in that part of the state ended earlier that spring and now she had to move north. Plus, she'd sufficiently trained the rest of the staff so she wouldn't have to return that way.

She'd made a promise.

"*Had to*" was the wrong connotation for what she would return north for. If she'd taken much longer than a year, Rachiah and Cyan would've been after her to get home anyway and they would've been much more forceful than the Bureau of Land Management.

And their compensation package wouldn't have been as persuasive.

The short drive to the office didn't cater to her melancholy. She'd packed up her last box at the apartment that morning. After she dropped her report off at the office, she could start her drive north.

To Taylor Falls, Clearwater County. Home. Where she had no one but her friends waiting for her.

Sherri pushed through the double-doors to the office building. She wouldn't miss the smell of burned popcorn that constantly pervaded the lower floors. But she would miss the easy access to the mulch for Tommy, and the constant access to crickets for his meals.

"Hey, girl. I'm going to miss you so much." Linda, with her shortly bitten nails and long stringy hair, rushed to throw her arms around Sherri's waist. "I brought in some doughnuts and milk with orange juice as a going away party. But… well, I think the guys got into them. There's only a couple maple bars left." She pulled away and shrugged apologetically. "Oh well, right? Us thick girls gotta watch our sugar." She winked, her garish mauve eyeshadow obliterating any hopes at being coy.

Smiling in agreement, Sherri swallowed her groan. *Thick.* Only women thought of her as fat or big-boned. The guys didn't have a problem with her curves.

Maybe that was the issue for the ladies.

Linda glanced over her shoulder as she returned to her receptionist desk. Tossing out a small laugh, she pointed at Sherri. "I mean, seriously, who ever *heard* of a fat vegan?" Her continued laughter scratched an already sensitive spot.

"Ha ha. Yeah." Sherri hurried on, transferring her clipboard from her hand to under her arm. Hopefully, no one else was in the office. Sherri needed one of those doughnuts like she needed a warm blanket in the middle of summer. But at the same time…

She needed to get home. The stress was lower, nothing pushed her, nothing challenged her. No one tried to make her fit into a specific spot. No one commented on her touching thighs or the fact that she sore something bigger than a size 8.

Her cellphone rang as she dropped the data-laden clipboard to the chipped desk in her soon-to-be-ex-boss's empty office. She didn't want to see anyone right then anyway.

Cyan's number flashed on the caller ID. Sherri would have to slip out the back to avoid Linda and anyone else.

She flipped open the phone and muttered, "Having cold feet yet? I'll be there in eight hours, I can spring you free." Only half-joking, Sherri ducked out the door, nothing left in the office for her to pack.

"Ha. Ha. Very funny. No, I wanted to make sure you're still coming. Rachiah tried canceling on me. I don't think that's funny." Cyan sounded less than amused.

"Why would she cancel? You're never getting married again – at least for the first time." Sherri smirked. She had to tease Cyan. If she didn't, who would?

Rounding the building and climbing into her small Nissan pickup, Sherri clenched her jaw. She'd drive through the night and barely get enough sleep the next day only to have to go out for Cyan's bachelorette party. She forced a smile. "I'll be there before you know it. We'll have lots of fun and I promise Rachiah is going." *If I am, she is.*

"Okay, thanks, Sher, I can't wait to see you. Drive carefully." Cyan hung up on Sherri briskly. Cyan would rather talk to Jareth anyway, than waste time with anyone else.

Sherri popped Tim McGraw's latest album into the CD player and buckled her seatbelt. She loved her truck. Her first sign of freedom, of responsibility.

She'd held down a job. An adult job, too. Not one of the fast food restaurant jobs. She actually had a job that used her degree.

The fact that she didn't feel anymore "adult" had to be in her head. She didn't need to jump into marriage like Cyan. Okay, Cyan wasn't *jumping* into anything. She and Jareth had been dating a while. Sherri got that. But she didn't need anyone to *save* her. She could take care of herself. She'd done it so far.

Plus, she couldn't wait to get home.

Heck, yeah, and she missed her friends. She just wasn't sure that the job and her friends were enough to liven up the small town feel of Taylor Falls.

The small town feel Sherri couldn't seem to shake.

~~~

Emma

Leaning on the counter of the bathroom, Emma closed her eyes. She was leaving out the makeup. Again. She just couldn't seem to get the energy up to put more of an effort in what she looked like.

Lately, her fatigue seemed to come from deep inside. Nate was home more to raise bison and work on the ranch, but that didn't take the stress off Emma.

If anything, as much as she loved her husband, Emma couldn't help feeling more pressure to always be *on*. Normally, when Hannah went to school and Stefanie was out doing all the things that she did between working and more schooling, Emma was able to take a nap in the middle of the afternoon. She had things she got done, but if she didn't want to eat, she didn't have to.

With Nate home more, there were more expectations to make sure dinner was on. When he was there, usually more of the family was, as well. Kyle and the Johnson boys all had monstrous appetites and expecting them to come in after working on the ranch to an empty table just wasn't acceptable.

Even if that meant she was falling asleep on the couch by Nate at seven o'clock, Emma was making dinner and working a lot more than she probably should be.

She sighed, pushing from the bathroom and rubbing at her lower back. Her pacemaker had given her a lot more energy. She refused to think anything else was wrong. She was just tired.

Everyone got tired. She couldn't think something was wrong just because of a little fatigue. Emma pulled her hair back into a ponytail and pasted a smile on her face as she descended the stairs. If someone was home and say how tired she was, they'd never let her live it down.

They might even tell Nate.

Hannah knew Emma was tired, but that was it. And Emma needed to keep it that way.

~~~

Sherri grabbed her last box of things and carried it into the small house she and Rachiah were renting together on the reservation. Rachiah's family, the Two-Claws, were letting them live there until the girls figured out what they were going to do from there.

Rachiah was supposed to arrive that afternoon. She better be there or Sherri would have to fill her throat with some fire ants. Or, maybe she would just imagine doing it.

"Wow, you have your vindictive look on." Cyan climbed the three cement steps to the front door and peeked inside. Her blue and yellow tie-dyed peasant shirt hung loosely over jeans and a collection of pearly beads dangled from her neck. She tucked a shock of blue hair behind her ear.

"Yeah, well, Rachiah's cutting it close." Sherri didn't feel like being magnanimous toward her friend.

She hadn't slept at all due to the road construction on I-90 causing a horrible traffic jam before the turnoff to Clearwater. She'd been stuck in that dang black truck in a road trap for three hours.

"She'll be here." Cyan smiled, swinging with one hand from the pole holding up the mini porch awning.

"Wow, your mood changed." Sherri's surly tone suggested she didn't like the adjustment at all. "I'd been counting on you being cranky with me."

"Nah, we're going out with the girls tonight. It's going to be *so* fun." Cyan tapped her watch. "You need to get dressed. We have to meet Emma, Hannah, and Stefanie for dinner."

Sherri paused with her foot half on and half off the top step "Wait, what? They're too young and that's really early. We weren't supposed to go out until later." There went her chance for a nap.

Cyan scrunched her nose. "I know. But Hannah and Stefanie wanted to do something and Emma can't go out late. She hasn't been feeling well. Remember,

I told you about her? She's been kind of run down lately, and Nate is nervous about her using too much energy." Cyan held up her hands, palms facing out. "But don't say anything. Nate doesn't want Emma thinking he's worried." She rolled her nose.

Right, the sister-in-law with the cancer. Sherri didn't mean to think so bluntly, but her fatigue wore at her. "I'm going to need some serious coffee. What are we doing after dinner?" She'd been counting on the free time to catch up on her sleep.

"Drinks in Colby. Rachiah has a friend who works at the bar down there. Said we might be able to get some karaoke going or something." She wiggled her eyebrows and smirked. "I know how much you *love* singing in front of others."

"Yeah, I'll drive separate." Sherri didn't want to be a poor sport, but she might not make it to the wedding the next day, if she didn't have enough sleep. Wasn't that more important than karaoke in Colby anyway?

Cyan stopped swinging around the pole and studied her friend. She nodded slowly. "Okay, I understand. We can follow each other. If you need to leave early, no stress, okay?" At least Cyan understood. She usually picked up when things weren't exactly perfect with Sherri or Rachiah. It was nice to have someone around that cared like Cyan did.

Her plan would work. If Sherri left early enough, maybe she wouldn't fall asleep at the wheel.

~~~

Emma leaned across the orange vinyl table cloth and offered the cardboard party hat to Sherri with a sympathetic shrug. "You get to wear this now, Sherri. I need to get going." She winked at Cyan and then Rachiah in turn. "It was nice seeing you girls again. I'll see you tomorrow at the ceremony." She held up a finger. "Wait, are you all coming to my place still to get ready beforehand?" She blinked, shadows under

31

her eyes speaking of the same exhaustion Sherri was trapped in.

Cyan glanced at Rachiah and Sherri, drawing her eyebrows together as she studied each of them. "I believe so, I left the dresses at Rachiah and Sherri's place." She'd claimed a chair at the end of the booth rather than squeeze into one of the bench seats with the girls.

"Sounds good." *Just go.* Sherri smiled enough to agree but not enough to spark another conversation. The sooner Emma and Nate's two sisters left, the sooner the rest of them could get on with their night and then head to bed. She really wasn't rude or mean, she just had a serious problem with large groups of people, especially those she didn't know well.

Sherri hadn't even had a chance to make her bed at the new place. She'd stacked her bedding on the mattress and stared at it longingly before leaving.

"We'll see you tomorrow, then." Emma smiled softly as she scooted out of the booth behind Stefanie and Hannah. Sweet girls. In fact, Sherri would love to spend time with them, when she wasn't so close to passing out and she hadn't missed Cyan and Rachiah as much as she had. Hannah was still too young to go to the bar, so even having her stay with them wasn't an option.

The bar right next door.

Cyan pointed toward the adjoining door and spoke to the waitress. "We're just going next door; can we move our tab?" She pulled cash out of her purse for a tip, and left it on the table while waiting for an answer.

Sherri tapped the table. "Aren't they owned by the same guy? I bet the tabs transfer easily."

The waitress followed Sherri who followed Rachiah who was led by the over-confident bride— bedecked out in her toilet paper bridal shower dress and glittery tiara. No one could say the group lacked class, even if it was trashy.

Sherri snorted at her inner dialogue. Oh, she was getting a little carried away. She had just eaten. A little coffee combined with over-fatigue. She wasn't the smartest sometimes. Now she was going to add alcohol to the mix? Yeah, she was looking for trouble.

"Oh, let's sit at the bar. We always sit at booths or tables." Cyan tugged Rachiah's arm and the tall black-haired Native American woman sent pleading glances toward Sherri as she allowed herself to be dragged toward the seats at the end of the counter.

Sherri scuffed her boots along the uneven planked flooring as she picked out a path behind them. There weren't too many people inside the dark interior of the bar. A man with a stained flannel wiped at the inner perimeter of the counter with an even more stained white-ish towel. But he manned a glass countertop that sparkled. He may have seemed unkempt but his work space was immaculate.

Sherri nodded shyly at his welcoming grin. She wasn't into new people, hardly at all and being at a bar on a Friday night didn't sit well with her introverted tendencies. She preferred bugs. Creatures with easy to understand needs and certainly fewer motives than the average person.

Cyan and Rachiah finally slid onto a set of seats and Sherri followed suit, claiming the stool with a plop and a sigh. She rubbed her eyes and stared blearily across from her into the bottle-blocked mirror, ignoring the shadows under her own eyes or the droopy lilt to her softly curled hair.

"Hey," He sidled up beside her, like his sunglasses would introduce him in the dark ambience as somehow cooler, somehow more desirable. His voice rolled off his tongue like a dose of cod liver oil with the bitter aftertaste. "You and your friends haven't been in here before." He slid his shades down his nose, displaying his studying beady eyes as he trailed his gaze on her from head to foot and then on to Rachiah and then Cyan.

Sherri glanced at her friends who were lost in conversation, bemoaning the loss of an autumn wedding and the fact that the temperature was supposed to be in the nineties the next day.

With no backup at the moment, Sherri couldn't get her mind to snap out of the haze her tiredness draped over her.

And when was the last time a guy had been interested in her? When had she been away from work? She wrapped her fingers around the glass the bartender placed in front of her. When had Cyan ordered her a cranberry vodka? Sherri's favorite. She smiled her thanks at the bartender and stirred the drink with the mini straw.

The bartender watched the man beside her. But while Sherri should've been flattered, she was still more tired than anything. Did she need someone to date? She wasn't exactly interested in romance or being wooed. She sipped her drink.

Not that the snake-charmer next to her was someone she'd ride into the sunset with.

Avoiding the man beside her and his creepy gaze, Sherri glanced around the interior of the dim bar. Neon signs blazed beside old-fashioned pictures framed in contemporary styles. Tall wooden backs separated the booths that lined the wall and standard rectangular tables manned the center of the room. A jukebox with CDs inside pulsed softly from the corner opposite the door.

An arresting man claimed a chair with the dominance of a well-fed mountain lion. He leaned his arm on the table beside him. His bright blue eyes landed on her and he narrowed his eyes as he watched her. He was more what she imagined her type to be – a brooding Mr. Darcy with a cowboy hat curved at the brim and a jawline tense with displeasure.

He didn't come her way or show any interest. Or show anything much beyond irritation. He nonchalantly left his ankle crossed over his knee, while giving off the aura that he was ready to pounce. On her? She couldn't be certain.

Still the salesman sat beside her, chattering like she didn't need to participate in the conversation.

She sipped more of her drink, the cold tartness a welcome relief after the increasingly let-down day.

Nodding at random points in the one-sided conversation, Sherri glanced again at the man sitting at the table. The intensity of his gaze brought goosebumps to her arms and she shivered. If she tried hard enough, would she be able to get him to interrupt? Probably not. The man beside her settled onto the stool beside her, essentially laying claim to the spot.

Great. Not what she wanted. And now, the man with the eyes probably wouldn't approach her, thinking she was taken or something.

Couldn't she get any of the good ones? She sighed and sipped her drink again. Since she wanted to drive soon, she wasn't going to drink much. Nothing needed to cloud her judgment with the car salesman next to her.

Chapter 2

Kyle

Kyle wasn't going to sit idly by while the reputation-ruining jerk destroyed another innocent woman. Guy Lansing prowled the watering holes like a dang predator, out to claim the least likely to protect herself.

He watched as Guy approached the trio and snagged onto the lagging friend on the end. The droop to her shoulders and the slouchy way she hung onto the bar suggested she was either already on her way to drunk or dejected in another manner.

Guy would pick up on any weaknesses like a coyote after the weak or old. He had those predator instincts.

Hadn't Kyle known that already with his sister, Ruby's experience? The experience was altogether too close for comfort as it was.

He curled his fingers tight to his palm, cutting his short nails into the fleshy part. No matter what, Guy wouldn't be allowed to take advantage of another girl against her will. At least if Kyle had anything to say about it.

Kyle watched the pair as she glanced his way. He couldn't help studying her.

She was exactly the type of girl Kyle tried to stay away from. Her doe eyes and soft hair held more appeal than any girl with heavy makeup and tight clothing could. Her curvy figure couldn't hide beneath her long sweater and jeans. She was more temptation than Kyle needed.

Maybe just once he wouldn't play hero – there might be more involved than just stopping a predator from making another victim. He needed to focus on continuing his plans for revenge. Jareth thought he was taking the big brother thing a little far, but then again, Jareth hadn't seen Ruby the morning after or taken her to the doctor a few weeks later.

Jareth wouldn't understand – because Kyle hadn't told him everything.

The woman at the bar half-shrugged at Guy and looked toward her friends who motioned toward the bathrooms and got up to leave her for a moment.

Kyle couldn't make out faces in the darkened interior or from his angle of seating. The woman nodded, her shoulders slumping more.

Guy claimed the opportunity with her back turned and put something into her drink, stirring it with his finger. Guy glanced around, furtively checking to see if anyone had seen.

Kyle had seen too much now *not* to be involved.

She didn't deserve that. No one deserved what Guy planned.

Motioning to the waitress that he wanted his check, Kyle stood to pull his wallet from his jeans. With one eye on the pair, Kyle paid his small tab, but the waitress dropped her tray, money falling to the floor.

Bending, Kyle swept the bills onto her tray and stood again. He retrained his gaze toward the couple. Alarmed, he stepped in that direction, his hand outstretched.

The girl was already sipping from her drink. Guy watched her hungrily and glanced past her for her friends every few seconds. Kyle had no doubt there were more drugs than necessary in the drink, so it wouldn't take long for them to take effect.

Normally, Kyle set up some kind of interruption with whichever bartender was on to get the girl away without Guy knowing Kyle was involved. But this time, Kyle hadn't acted fast enough. And he didn't know *that* particular bartender since Kyle and the rest of the Trails never been in Colby long enough before. Sure, they'd skirted Taylor Falls and half the other towns in Clearwater County, but Colby was a new one for he and his cousins to work in for any length of time – at least since the beginning.

Alarmed that he might be too late, Kyle rushed the final distance to the woman's side and wrapped an arm around her shoulders for the potential need for support. As soon as Guy got his arms around her, Kyle would have a harder time saving her. "You okay, darlin'?" She smelled more like citrus which was a refreshing change from the musty odor of the bar like spilled alcohol and stale peanuts.

She glanced up at him, her brown eyes more like caramel than the dark chocolate he'd envisioned. Nodding, she blinked as her eyelids drooped. "Yes, thank…" She sagged against him, her weight pushing on his chest.

Training his steely gaze on Guy, Kyle lifted his chin. "Working on your next victim, Guy?" He didn't let the woman go. If he did, she'd certainly collapse to the floor. "How much did you put in that drink, this time?" She was out a lot faster than Kyle would have expected for the small amount she'd had.

The thin man jerked back, his sunglasses slipping from his nose to dangle from one ear while he lifted his hands like a shield. "Darby. What are you doing here? I thought you were up around White Fish this season." H said the last with accusation in his tone.

"You'd like that, wouldn't you, worthless weasel." Kyle glared at the man who shifted his gaze between his female target and her would-be rescuer.

Guy's worry turned to smugness. "Oh, I see. You want to claim her. You're letting me do all the work and you swing in to reap the benefit. I get it. Okay." He winked and leaned forward, punching Kyle on the

upper arm. "Next time, I'll find a duo for us to share –
" He yanked backwards at the anger simmering in
Kyle's growl.

"I'm going to follow you everywhere. I'll be at
every bar, at every party you go to. You might not be
able to see me, but I'll be there, watching you."
Kyle's voice rumbled from deep in his chest with
unrequited fury he struggled to maintain. "If this
happens again, I'm going to find a place to put your
body where no one will ever think to look."

Kyle thrusted his jaw toward the door, everything
in him demanding that he lay into the snake but the
gentleman in him refused to drop the woman. "Go on.
Git." Guy didn't even take the time to scowl before
scampering out the exit like a dog with his tail
between his legs.

"Thanks, man. I had my suspicions, but nothing
concrete. This is the fourth time he's been in here this
week." The bartender slid a bottle of Moose Drool, a
dark huckleberry ale, across the bar to Kyle. "This
one's on me."

Leaning his head to the side, Kyle peeked at his current damsel-in-distress. "Thanks, I appreciate it. Wait a minute. Is she sleeping?"

Her light brown hair hung across her face, softly moving with the puffs of air from her nose as she breathed.

"Appears so." The bartender tapped the counter. "The other two spilled something. They should be right back. This one drove her own rig from what they were saying. You look familiar, you one of them Trails working out at the Jonesy ranch?" He moved as if to round the counter, motioning to the four people at the end of the bar who walked up to order.

"Yeah, I'm standing foreman." Kyle nodded, his hat dipping and lifting.

Nodding, the bartender pulled open Sherri's small purse dangling from her shoulder and dug until he produced a small ring of keys. "Can I help you get her outside?"

Kyle glanced at the keys then back at the girl. "Nah, it's okay. What color is her car?"

Passing the keys to Kyle, the bartender arched an eyebrow with a side-smile. "Color doesn't matter. It's the only Nissan for miles around."

Nissan, huh? What was wrong with a Ford or Chevy? Nothing wrong with Dodge either – heck, at least you could trust a Dodge owner. You didn't have to agree with their obviously wrong choice but at least you could trust 'em.

"Thanks. I can do it. I'll be back in a bit." He hefted her into his arms, her solid form fitting against him like they'd been created to match up.

The bartender slapped the counter twice. "I'll tell her friends you got her out of here so they don't worry about her."

Only Kyle couldn't ignore the soft scent of citronella and oranges coming off her skin. She was intoxicating and he hadn't even spoken to her. She was going to be more dangerous for him, then he'd originally supposed.

Leaning backwards a bit, Kyle strode across the bar and carried her through the doors, pushing with his hips to get outside. He took less than a moment to locate the shiny Nissan pickup in the parking spot along the street.

Close to the bar. Perfect. He started toward the side of the truck. Beside the driver side door, he allowed her feet to carefully slide to the ground to help rest some of her weight on the floor. He opened the door and shifted her inside.

Movement caught his eye from across the street and just outside the circles of light cast down by the streetlights Guy waited. His beady eyes glinted as he moved. He watched Kyle. Or was he watching the girl to see what would happen?

Kyle glanced at the building. Did he take the chance to dart inside and tell her friends? Or would it be better to get her out of there and somewhere safe before coming back and getting her friends? The bartender had assured him he'd pass on the information. Kyle would have to trust that he would.

His gaze darted to where Guy had hidden in the shadows. Kyle's worry mounted as he realized he had no idea where Guy had slipped off to. No. He was going to have to get into the truck. He buckled the girl in and shut the door carefully to make sure she stayed inside the cab but nothing was going to get caught in the door.

Everything was going to crap. Nothing was sticking to routine. Kyle never had this kind of trouble trying to save a girl from Guy. Why now? Why today?

The sudden disappearance of the rapist worried Kyle enough to push away his need to tell her friends and just get her the heck out of there.

Rounding the front of the truck, Kyle opened the front door and slid inside. Kyle would have to call his brother and let him know he didn't need a ride back from Colby. Knowing Kyle would most likely need to have the unnamed girl drive him to the ranch the next day – hopefully before the wedding, Kyle could at least assure his brother he'd be fine. Plus, she shouldn't be too put off by that. He hoped.

He glanced at the girl leaning against the window as he adjusted her in the bench seat. He closed the driver's side door and turned the key he'd taken from the bartender in the ignition. Well, he had no idea where he was going. All he knew was he couldn't stay there with that girl and Guy lurking around.

If she didn't wake soon to tell him where she lived, they'd be sleeping at a camp along the side of the road. He couldn't take her to the ranch bunkhouse and he couldn't afford a hotel.

He didn't have any other choice. He had to wake her up. Maybe he could wake her up enough to get directions to her place or at least an idea of which direction to head.

Leaning across the seat, Kyle gently shook her shoulder. "Excuse me, are you awake? Hello?" He jostled her again and sighed in relief as she fluttered her eyes open. He spoke softer, but loud enough to get her attention. "Where do you live? I need to get you home."

She groaned and tried lifting her hand only to have it fall to her side. She blinked at him, slowly like her eyelids were weighted down. She turned her face back and sighed. "Um, I'm at the Two-Claw cabin… um… Reser…" Her eyes slid shut and her breathing deepened. She mumbled, "Pretty eyes."

Straightening, Kyle considered her. Had she been talking about his eyes or Guys? More concerning was her description of her home. Grimly pulling from the curb, Kyle pursed his lips. That late at night on the reservation? Hopefully, he could get onto the reservation without being spotted. Their circumstances were extremely suspicious and he'd have a hard time explaining things to the Redhawks.

Hopefully, she told the truth. Kyle would hate to drive onto the reservation and have nowhere to go. That'd be guaranteed danger.

He pinched the bridge of his nose. The girl was already shaping up to be more trouble than Kyle had bargained for.

If he got her to her place and then couldn't get off the land, he'd be in no better position. Some things you walked away from. He should have walked away.

~~~

Cyan

Cyan giggled as she straightened her makeshift veil and glanced back at Rachiah following her from the scarred and worn ladies' room. She rolled her eyes. "I don't care what it actually is, you look like you wet your pants." She tossed a swift peek at the wet spot on Rachiah's jeans and laughed again.

Exasperated, Rachiah shook her head and gripped Cyan's shoulders from behind and redirected her toward the bar. "It was orange juice. We didn't need to make a bigger mess trying to get it out of my pants. I think you did it on purpose." She let go of Cyan's shoulders and scanned the bar, pointing at the empty seat they'd left Sherri in. "Hey, where'd Sherri go?"

Sobering rather quickly, Cyan blinked and looked at the barstool they'd left her friend at. If she stared hard enough, would Sherri suddenly appear? Not likely. She slowly spun around, taking in the rest of the bar's occupants as much as she could in the dim interior. At the end of the counter, the bartender spoke with a new group of people as he pointed at the menu in their hands.

Biting her inner lip, Cyan moved to the doorway and glanced out at the street. Sherri had parked on the road, in the only now-empty spot. She furrowed her brow and turned back to Rachiah who had followed her to the door. "Her truck is gone. She must have gone home."

"But without telling us? That doesn't seem like Sherri. And that guy she was with? Where'd he go?" Rachiah turned back to the bar, approaching it with long strides and a purpose. She leaned against the counter, bracing her hands on either side of her waist as she stared at the bartender until he left the group and approached them.

Eyebrow cocked, he shook his head, pointing at Sherri's empty seat. "She was in a lot of trouble with that guy." He reached down, claiming his ever-dirty appearing rag and rinsing it out in the behind-the-counter sink. Wringing it out, he nodded toward the door. "Another guy took her home."

Cyan's jaw fell open. "She just went with him? Some random guy? Sherri isn't like that at all." Cyan's chest rose and fell as she grew slightly panicked. What had happened to Sherri? Was she going to end up dead in a ditch?

The bartender shook his head and reached out, patting the counter in front of Cyan's empty glass. "The guy she was sitting with didn't take her home. He was scared off by a local ranch hand we have here in town. From what I understand, he's a good guy. I don't know him personally, but his reputation precedes him. He's the foreman out at Jonesy's ranch. He said she'd get home. I have no doubt she'll get there." He tilted his head toward Cyan's drink. "Would you like another?"

Cyan glanced at Rachiah. Would she like another drink? The look in her friend's gaze suggested that she was probably done for the night. Cyan didn't blame her. She was tired, too.

And she had a big day ahead of her. She shook her head and pulled out her wallet. "No, thank you. I think we're ready to head back home. What's the damage?"

As she paid the bill, she couldn't help thinking it was the last time she'd pay with *her* money as a single woman. After the next day, everything would be *theirs*.

Cyan couldn't be more excited.

Chapter 3

Sherri

Had she fallen asleep with a mouthful of wood crammed on her tongue? Sherri worked her throat but the slight movement combined with blinking too quickly shoved a wave of dizziness into her ears like q-tips.

She squeezed her eyes shut harder, wincing at the over-sensitivity. Inhaling deep through her nose, she slowly opened her eyelids like she was worried about being jabbed.

The sun wasn't over bright which didn't mean anything since Sherri's bedroom window faced north. *Thank Heaven*.

Sitting up, she glanced around her new-yet-to-be-used bed. She hadn't changed, had in fact slept in the clothes she'd worn out with the girls. Wait a minute. She hadn't made her bed either, but there she was lying on top of a comforter tucked neatly over her sheets and her covered pillow. Maybe she'd come home and made the bed? Doubtful. She didn't remember much of anything.

Except for the eyes. Boy, did she remember the *eyes*.

Great. She'd never hear the end of it from the girls. Getting trashed wasn't Sherri's thing. It wasn't any of their "thing". So, the very rare times it happened, the person didn't live it down for a long time.

The tinkling of glass in the kitchen made her hang her head. She'd definitely hear about it from Rachiah. Good thing Sherri hadn't slept in long enough to miss the wedding.

She snapped her head up, thrusting herself from the bed and rushing toward the hall. Her nervous adrenaline pushed aside the inevitable nausea, but the headache was a new one. She gritted her teeth at the effects of the hangover and gripped her hands into fists at her sides.

The wedding! How much time did Sherri have?

Rubbing at her eyes, she covered the hallway with a few strides. "How long do we have? I didn't mean to fall asleep last night. Thanks for getting me home, 'Chiah." Sherri stopped at the doorway to the small kitchen and dining room combo.

Rachiah wasn't standing at the stove.

No, some guy with jeans and no shirt and bare feet stood with a hip against the counter, sipping a chipped mug of coffee.

At least the fragrance hinted at coffee.

Damp dark auburn hair fell across his forehead. "Mornin'." His drawl was long and drawn out as he took in her disheveled appearance, amusement in the small dimple in his whiskered cheek.

Sherri's mouth fell open. She glanced around at Rachiah's closed bedroom door. "Um…" She tried not to stare at his well-defined pecs and abs and shoulders… wow, those shoulders… but it was hard.

The play on words made her giggle. She was out of her gourd. She blinked a couple times. His eyes. They were so familiar. So blue.

She pointed toward her friend's door. "I'm sorry. Is Rachiah coming out soon?" One-night stands weren't Rachiah's thing either, but from the looks of the cowboy standing in the kitchen, he'd be a strong temptation for anyone to get a new habit.

He cocked an eyebrow at her and lowered his mug. "Rachiah?"

Sherri scoffed, rolling her eyes. "You should probably know someone's name before you go home with them, don't you think?" She crossed to her purse lying haphazardly on the floor under the table.

"Rachiah? Okay, third person, that's weird but okay, I'll play. How did Rachiah sleep? Kyle didn't sleep so well, but Rachiah kicks a lot in bed." He winked and smiled knowingly.

Swinging her purse over her shoulder, Sherri screwed her lips to the side. "Ew, I don't want to know what you two did." She rapped her knuckles on Rachiah's door panel, giving Kyle the once-over and continued, "Rachiah, time to get up, girl. Your date is a little creepy."

"Wait, you're not Rachiah? Then who are *you*?" He set the cup down and crossed the linoleum floor to stand in front of her. His muscles flexed as he moved and Sherri avoided staring directly at his chest.

Or tried to appear like she wasn't staring. *Okay, forget it.* She stared, slowly dragging her gaze to his mesmerizing eyes. She cleared her throat. "I'm Sherri. Rachiah's roommate. I don't remember you coming home with her last night." She couldn't admit that she didn't remember much of anything last night after the oily man started talking to her.

"You wouldn't remember that since I didn't." He winked and pointed his finger at her like he held his hands in a gun shape. "I came home with *you*. Sherri." He walked back toward her bedroom, humming as he sauntered away.

Why did he wear it like a crown and she felt like she'd just done the walk of shame?

Shock held her back for a split second, then she rushed after him. "Wait, what?" Not possible. She didn't go home with random men. Even if they did look like Kyle.

Inside her bedroom door, he bent to pick up his shirt but jerked his hand to his waist. The sudden tension in his back muscles probably held in a silent scream for how fast he recoiled to the opposite wall.

"Don't move!" He held his hand toward her to stop her coming into the room.

"What? Oh my gosh, what is it?" She angled her head around his arm. Nothing unusual caught her eye. Tommy crawled across a flannel shirt thrown over a pile of boxes. At least Tommy was safe. She signed in relief. She took inventory of her unpacked room. Nothing alarming stood out to her. "What?"

He whispered out of the side of well-sculpted lips. "There's a huge spider walking toward us. Do. Not. Move."

Sherri's eyes widened and she stared between Kyle and Tommy. The seriousness of the situation wasn't lost on her as she ducked under Kyle's arm. "He's more afraid of you, than you are of him." She leaned down and slowly coaxed Tommy onto her palm. She pierced Kyle with her gaze. "Please, don't tell me those big bad muscles are hiding one huge baby." She arched her eyebrows in challenge as the soft silky legs of her tarantula tickled the palm of her hand.

Kyle's chest moved up and down in a jerky rhythm. He held his hands to the sides, palms up. "Um, he's going to bite you and I don't know where the closest hospital is. You'll be dead before we get to your truck."

Sherri crossed to Tommy's cage and placed him inside with care. She replaced the lid and flipped on his sun light. "There you go. You need to stop getting out. There's nothing for you out here."

Then she turned, unable to contain her laughter any further. "Are you serious with that? He's a tarantula. He's not going to bite you. Not poisonous either. Most spiders don't have the right anatomical structuring to bite us – it'd be like us trying to bite a wall." She giggled, still seeing in her mind how his fear had tightened his facial muscles and clenched his back like a tight rubber band.

The absence of answering humor on his face sobered Sherri immediately. She stepped forward until she was close enough to place her hand on his forearm. "I'm sorry. It's really not funny that you're scared. I'm just not used to a big strong man reacting like that…" Her voice trailed off. She didn't have the words to make her reaction to his fear okay.

She tried not focusing on the rippling strength beneath her fingers or the heat emanating from his bare skin. "It's not funny. Most people don't like spiders. I'm more afraid of fire than I am bugs." She shrugged. "Everyone's different."

Then reality hit her. "Wait, you stayed here last night? In my room? With *me*?"

There was nowhere else to sleep. They didn't have a couch yet and the floor wasn't exactly a hospitable place to expect him to sleep, but she didn't go home with guys. That wasn't her. She swallowed. "I don't… I'm sorry. I'm not sure what… happened."

He stared at her and then humor finally washed his fear away. "Now *that's* funny. Darlin', when I take you to bed, you'll remember it. Actually, I drove you here because the scumbag hitting on you slipped something into your drink. He's the worst type of creature and I didn't think it would be fair to let you fall victim to that." He ran his hands through his thick hair. "And for the record, I like spiders just fine. I'm just not accustomed to seeing one the size of a duck on my shirt."

Sickened that the man had tried drugging her, Sherri picked up Kyle's shirt and handed it to him. How could someone do that? *Don't look at Kyle's stomach or his chest – don't do it, Sherri. Crap, you did it.*

"You didn't drink enough to get plastered. My guess is there was enough drug in there for a full glass and you had less than a fourth remaining. You probably had a much stronger dose than you should've." He drew his shirt on like he had an idea what the sight of his muscles did to women.

His kindness overthrew her and she stared at him a moment. "Well, thank you. That was very chivalrous of you." That combined with the intensity of his blue gaze and she couldn't help the small crush building in her chest.

But she wasn't a damsel-in-distress. She didn't need help. The fact that he'd helped her, saved her from a fate she didn't want to think about, irked her just enough to raise her hackles.

He glanced around. "No problem. Listen, is it okay if I borrow your phone? My battery's dead." He jerked his thumb toward the hallway. "I don't usually have a phone on me, but my brother makes me take one when I go… out."

It took a moment for Sherri to register what he said. "Oh, yes, of course." She pulled out the cell from her purse. A green blinking light on the face of her phone drew her eye. "I have some missed messages. Just a second."

Two from Rachiah.

The first one had come in the night before.

Glad that cowboy took you home. Bartender said who he was. Get some sleep, I'll probably sleep over at Cyan's. She's freaking out with nerves.

The second one had come in just moments before.

Where are you? Cy will kill you if you're not here in the next ten minutes! You better not be dead in a ditch somewhere! She'll never let me come get you.

Sherri squinted at the clock. "Oh my gosh, is it really that late? I need to go." She tossed the phone at Kyle, rushing around the room as she gathered up the dresses Cyan had left at their place. All of the dresses were there. Cyan's, Rachiah's, Sherri's, and Emma's. No one had their dresses because of Sherri.

She didn't have time to drool over the hot cowboy any further. She had to rush around and get in the truck for survival.

Nothing was scarier than Cyan on a rampage.

Chapter 4

Kyle

Kyle handed the phone to Sherri, or tried to as she scrambled around the small house like a tornado with curves. "I called my brother. He's going to be here in a little bit."

She stopped long enough to narrow her eyes at him. "I have nothing to steal, so I'll just leave you here. I have to leave like three hours ago. Make yourself at home until he gets here. Thank you again." She shifted awkwardly on her feet, bobbing toward him and back and close and back like she might kiss his cheek or something in an awkward dance.

"See you 'round." Kyle awkwardly clasped her fingers in his and pumped their joined hands once, twice and dropped hers.

She wiggled her fingers in the air toward him, scooping the dress bags into her arms and rushing out the door.

Puffing air up toward his forehead, Kyle ran his fingers through his hair. What had just happened? He'd been so worried she'd turn into one of those girls you couldn't get rid of with clingy phone calls and pleas for you to stay all day.

Instead, she'd turned out to be the woman he couldn't get to sit down for two seconds. Of course, the one time he was interested in getting to know her better, she wasn't on board.

True, he couldn't stay long. His brother was getting married and wasn't amused at the extra trip to get him. Jareth didn't trust any of the other guys to come grab him though. So, Kyle would take his irritation when he arrived.

Kyle wandered back into the kitchen and rinsed his coffee mug. He emptied the other coffee cup into the sink.

He'd taken a shower and watched her sleep in a purely non-creepy way. Why hadn't he seen the spider?

How emasculating. She'd had to protect him from her pet.

Her pet tarantula.

Kyle couldn't deny how much that added to her attraction. A girl that was into spiders? A girl that wasn't afraid of much. She didn't even freak out over the drugging incident, even though she had every reason to and would be justified in doing so. A girl with no fear? Something he was definitely interested in.

He didn't want to like anyone. He'd known the second he saw her at the bar, she would be trouble for him.

Dang girl and her spider.

~~~

"Hey, Jareth. You look like you're ready for a funeral." Kyle smirked as he climbed into his brother's old school truck. The brown rig had become like a second brother to Kyle. Sometimes more reliable than his own since Jareth had found Cyan, but only a few minutes with her charm and Kyle couldn't begrudge Jareth any of the time he spent with his bride-to-be.

Jareth scowled. "Yeah, if we're late, we'll be going to my funeral. Might as well dress

75

appropriately." The black tuxedo and bolo style tie lent an air of Houston-cowboy to the man. His black cowboy hat and black boots shined with newness.

Kyle whistled as he slammed his door shut. "Wow, Cyan made you get matching digs, huh? That's crazy. Those Stetsons aren't cheap."

Jareth shrugged, backing his truck out of the driveway. "Whatever she wants, Kyle. I don't care. She needs to be happy. Plus, she has the money to afford it." His face softened as he talked about his girl. The juxtaposition of the two of them together had a surprising twist as Jareth and Cyan adjusted to each other and their expectations.

Kyle loved seeing his brother happy – he'd just never admit it to anyone.

A siren rang out behind them along with flashing lights.

Jareth glared at Kyle, clenching his jaw. He lifted his hand and closed his eyes for a second. "Great, Redhawks."

"Nah, that's just Rez police." Kyle angled around, straining for a sign that he was right. *Please, let me be right.*

"Nope, that's M.T. Crap." Jareth rolled down his window, his smile tight. As the raven-haired man approached, Jareth lifted his hand. "Hello, M.T. how're things? Was I speeding?"

M.T., the leader of the Redhawks on the reservation, focused on Jareth then searched Kyle's face just past him. He inclined his head, his regality never lowered. "No. You weren't. Why are you here? This is my sister's place. My parent's place. What are you doing here?" He narrowed his eyes, a feather tied in his hair fluttered when he stood in complete stillness. "Sherri just left."

Jareth pointed at Kyle. "Yeah, my kid-brother made sure she made it home last night. He said something on the phone about some guy trying to roofie her." He motioned toward his clothes. "I'm getting married and I came to pick him up, but

Cyan… well." He sighed, tilting his head and shrugging.

M.T. lifted his eyebrows, moving to rest his hand on the windowsill of the truck. "You're marrying Cyan? You better not be late. That girl is high strung sometimes." He nodded toward Kyle. "Thanks for taking care of Sherri. She's like family. We'll watch her from now on." His tone suggested more than the gratitude his words declared. More like a *"don't worry about her anymore, we got this"* kind of thing.

Kyle jerked his agreement. Really, why hadn't he put two and two together? He'd known Cyan had a friend named Rachiah who was Native American from the Salish reservation.

But he'd never met her other friend, only heard about her in passing as the bug girl. A lot of things were starting to make sense.

M.T. patted the side of the truck as he walked away.

"Apparently we've been excused?" Kyle's bitterness ate at his mood. He hadn't planned on seeing Sherri again, hadn't known it was even possible. He knew where she lived, but he worked and didn't have plans on starting anything.

But there he was, driving toward a wedding they would both be at.

Wasn't that where girls were more open to romances? Just because she'd zoomed out of his life and didn't seem interested didn't mean she wasn't. She probably never thought they'd see each other again either.

How would she react to seeing him?

The twist in emotions and possibilities intrigued him. Kyle tapped the cracked vinyl of the arm rest on the door beside him. He suddenly couldn't wait to get to the wedding.

~~~

M.T.

Pulling out his cell, M.T. slid into the driver's seat of his rig and rested his elbow on the window ledge. He punched in some numbers and pressed *call.*

After the fourth ring, a man on the other end answered. M.T. didn't waste time on pleasantries. "I'm not sure where Sherri was at last night, but I want you to find out. I want you to figure out who was trying to drug her and I want that name on my phone in the next twelve hours. Then we'll gather the posse." He didn't need to fill in more than that.

There were expectations from his family, from his community. Protecting friends was one of them. The alarm that had twisted in his gut at the Trails' comment had made Maverick catch his breath. Sherri had been roofied. At least that guy had been there to bring her home safely.

M.T. would never forgive himself, if she'd been hurt in any way. He would have to step on things, gather his courage, if he wanted to be in a position where it was his right to take care of her, his right to protect her, his right to call her his own.

He hung up the phone without anything more. He'd delivered his directions. They'd be followed. The honor of the Blackhawks demanded it.

~~~

Kyle

"Run out back and get changed. Your suit's in the barn hanging up. I gotta grab the guys for pictures. Cyan's parents want all the photos they can get." Jareth rolled his eyes and jumped from his parked truck. "Get there as soon as you can. I'm not joking."

Following Jareth's example, albeit at a slower speed, Kyle climbed from the truck, looking around.

Nate and Emma's place had been turned out with white folding chairs set up to create an outdoor audience. Blue tie-dyed tablecloths covered the reception area separated from the ceremony area with large overhead canopies. Beautiful hyacinth bouquets draped from the backs of chairs. Daisy rings hung from hooks at each pole of the tents and along the barns. Sashes dyed to match the tablecloths draped on anything that wasn't covered in flowers or some other decoration.

No expense had been spared.

How in the heck had Cyan turned out so unspoiled with parents who threw money at her like they did?

Kyle caught Jareth's gaze and shrank at the implied threat in his brother's eyes. Kyle held up his hands and mouthed, "I'm going." Rushing to the rear of the barn, he pulled on the tuxedo his brother had gotten him and ignored the Stetson hanging beside it. He'd wear his own hat, thank you very much.

If his luck held, he'd get to see the bug girl. He couldn't wait to see her reaction at seeing him at the wedding. If he hadn't expected it, why would she?

Chapter 5

Sherri

Sherri pushed through the doors at Emma's place and didn't get a chance to explain the last twelve hours.

Cyan rushed her, grabbing the dress bag and squeezing it to her chest. "Oh, my goodness, Sherri. Are you okay?" She recoiled. "Peew, you stink like that bar. Go take a fast shower. We're doing braids so your hair doesn't need to be dry. Rachiah, can you help Emma with her dress?" She waved Sherri off and spun toward the front living room. "Bathroom is up the stairs, Sherri."

And with that, Sherri was dismissed. She was just tired enough that she snarled at Rachiah when she passed. Immediately afterward, she felt bad. It wasn't their fault she felt like she'd been dragged backward through the desert and left out to dry for the bugs to nip at.

She had to let it go. This was her best-friend's special day. Sherri had to let go of her own issues and focus on the matter at hand.

Taking a deep breath, she made her way to the bathroom and climbed into the shower after shedding her clothes. *Okay, no big deal. No stress.* She'd probably feel better after a shower. Obviously a fast one or she'd push Cyan from relieved to… Bucking Bronco Bride.

Nobody wanted that.

~~~

The ends of her braids darkened the top of her ice blue bridesmaid dress. She didn't hate it and she didn't love it. The A-line skirt bit into her waist and the half-sleeves enhanced the size of her arms, which of course were one of her least favorite parts of her body.

"Oh, you girls look so sweet." Cyndi, Cyan's mom, walked through the front door, her hands folded at her chest. She beamed at the gathered bridesmaids.

Rachiah wore a darker shade of blue as the maid of honor.

"The groomsmen will be ready shortly. They will pair with you at the start of the path. Please, stay with your partner throughout the pictures." Cyndi smiled as she passed the women, tears in her eyes. She looked around the cluttered living room and hallway.

Opening her hands in question, she called out, "Okay, Cyan, where are you?"

At the end of the hallway, Cyan replied, "I'm coming. Just a sec." Swishing announced her arrival. Her dress moved, whispering around her legs as she came down the steps.

Her long white dress complete with beading and a softly modest neckline created the picture-perfect princess appearance. Three-quarter length sleeves ended above a small henna tattoo on one arm, matching the one on Cyndi's forearm.

Cyndi sobbed softly, rushing toward her daughter who was the picture of every girl's dream.

Sherri forgot why she'd been cranky. Suddenly seeing her friend dressed like a fairy princess dropped the magic of the wedding over her like a cloud. She sighed at the romance.

Rachiah's cheeks glowed and she smiled at Sherri, grabbing her hands as she bounced forward on her heels. "I'm so excited. Do you think M.T. will make it?"

Holding her smile steady, Sherri certainly hoped not. M.T., or Maverick, was Rachiah's older brother and he'd crushed on Sherri for as long as she could remember. She'd turned him down the last hundred times he'd asked her out.

Not that she had anything against Maverick. He was a good-looking guy and nice as they could get, but come on. She wasn't interested in dating her "brother" and that's exactly how it would feel if she went out with M.T. He'd want to kiss or something and, just, ew, no. He was the only person in the world who had witnessed just how afraid of fire she really was.

The wedding coordinator cut in before Sherri had to answer. "Ladies, let's get going. We'll be doing pictures following the ceremony. The Burns were kind enough to hire multiple photographers to make that part go fast. We would like to avoid the heat as much as possible, but we need you to stay away from the misters until after the pictures. Water spots are not pretty on film." She winked, a pencil shoved behind her ear and a little bit of pink lipstick on her front tooth.

Emma would go first to match up with Nate who was one of the groomsmen. They had to arrange that in case she got dizzy walking the distance to the front. No one was admitting to Emma that they knew she wasn't doing great, but they all treated her with kid gloves.

Sherri would go next and was paired with one of the cousins. "What was my guy's name?" She grabbed up a fistful of dress and lifted it above her feet to walk.

"Ryland Johnson." Rachiah winked. "I have Jareth's brother. He's taller than me, so that shouldn't be a problem." She'd worn flat sandals to avoid any issues with her height. But her long legs didn't let anyone else deny how tall she really was.

Sherri secretly envied her, but her longtime friend was nothing but nice and loyal – those characteristics didn't lend themselves to a jealous feeling. Plus, where would Sherri be without her friends? She adored them. It wasn't their fault Sherri was round in places she'd rather not be.

Following Emma out the door and to the deck, Sherri stepped carefully in the shoes she'd been given to wear. She would've preferred hiking boots and was actually surprised Cyan hadn't let them all go barefoot.

Emma swayed at the top of the steps, smiling gratefully when Sherri discreetly slipped her arm through hers. "Thanks. I'm not usually this tired."

"It's fine. This way I'm not walking alone. It was not a night I'm recovering from easily." Sherri winked and they took the steps one at a time. Following the trail of daisy heads, the two women stopped at the start of the aisle.

Turning, Emma waited for Nate who grabbed a blond man by the arm and they rushed over to stand beside Emma and Sherri.

Nate studied Emma's face. "Are you okay? Is she okay?" He turned his piercing gaze to Sherri, his intensity complete. His suit almost shining in the blazing sun.

Sherri looked to Emma. "Um, I think so? She seemed fine walking over. I mean, I'm shakier than she is."

Meeting Sherri's gaze gratefully, Emma swatted at Nate's hand softly. "Nate, don't scare her. Let's get down the aisle. I'm so excited for Cyan and Jareth." But she looked more worn than anything with shadows under her eyes and her braids accentuating the sharp angle to her cheeks.

Concern darkened Nate's gaze. "Okay, let's go. Take it slow, though, alright?" He only had eyes for his wife as he carefully placed her hand on his arm and they stepped down the aisle with the start of the violin playing a beautiful Simon and Garfunkel piece.

Sherri grinned, shaking her head. Simon and Garfunkel in a region of the world where they liked their music sang with a guitar and chaw in their bottom lip.

"That's a beautiful grin to wear with a gorgeous gown." The tall blond man with shoulders that spread forever stood before Sherri with his arm offered at an angle. He arched his light eyebrows over blue eyes that matched the clear sky. "Shall we?"

"Ryland? The cousin?" Sherri couldn't hold in her smile. She'd have to thank the wedding coordinator later. What was her luck? Two gorgeous cowboys in the same morning?

Every entomologist's dream.

"That's me. I'm *the* cousin. Or one of many." He winked and nodded.

Sherri took his arm and they fell into step, matching the pace of Nate and Emma who walked about twenty feet above them. The grass aisle lent an air of informality to the ceremony, a touch of freshness where a church or indoors might have stifled the excitement on the air. Every time the breeze stirred, a fresh scent of flowers flitted around them.

Eyes forward, Sherri whispered to Ryland, "This is the longest aisle ever. Do you think they'll have a spot halfway down we can stop and eat lunch?" Right in that moment she realized she hadn't had breakfast. With a brand-new home and no chance to shop and then of course sleeping in and waking to one of the best-looking men ever in her kitchen, Sherri didn't have much opportunity to think of food.

But her hunger hit her right then and she glanced around for something that might pass as lunch. Or even edible.

Ryland's deep laugh warmed Sherri. He leaned over, glancing at the crowd staring as they passed. "I doubt that, but I think we should request it at our wedding."

Sherri jerked back, his comment taking her by surprise.

"I'm joking. Just joking." He patted her hand and smiled around at the audience. "Look, I see an end in sight. Emma and Nate just parted at the front."

"Aw, frass." Sherri glanced between him and the spectators, unsure about his easy-going attitude and familiar tone even though they'd just met. She didn't let her smile wan though and held up appearances as they continued their trek. She was fine with teasing, but there was joking around and then there was intentional flirting.

She wasn't good at the latter.

He shot her a quizzical look at her phrase usage but didn't drop his smile.

At the end, she gratefully separated from Ryland's arm and turned to walk to the spot beside

Emma. Taking her place to stand in front of Emma but to the side, Sherri watched as the heads of the crowd swiveled to watch Rachiah traipse between them on the arm of a very tall, very auburn, very observant Kyle.

Kyle. Her Kyle? Not the Kyle who had been in her kitchen that morning. Wait. He wasn't *her* Kyle, per se.

Looked like it. And he watched Sherri with a side grin that suggested they shared a secret.

Judging by the smirk, their secret was much naughtier from his perception than Sherri's. She couldn't help returning the grin with a partial smile and a slight shake of her head.

So, that was Jareth's brother. What were the odds she'd find the guy who was very clearly off-limits? Or maybe wasn't. She wasn't sure. But brothers of her friends just didn't sit right in the whole realm of interest.

Besides, just because she was interested, didn't mean he was.

Plus, he was the only groomsmen wearing a dark brown Stetson, the rest wore the standard black.

Leave it to Sherri to have eyes for the guy who didn't conform.

Chapter 6

Kyle

Kyle knew the second Sherri recognized him. Of course, he enjoyed it and let her know with a teasing grin.

He split from Rachiah and moved to stand beside Ryland, crossing his hands in front of him as he waited for Cyan to walk down the aisle toward his brother.

Embarrassed at the tears in Jareth's eyes, he focused on just getting through the proceedings.

Until Kyle got a good look at the happiness on Cyan's face. If he could make someone that happy to see him, to walk toward forever with him, he'd probably weep, too.

During the handoff from Mr. Burns to Jareth, Ryland leaned over, eyes focused forward and whispered, "Man, Cyan has some hot friends, right?" The direction of his gaze made it hard to figure out which friend he was talking about specifically.

Did he mean Rachiah?

Or was he thinking Sherri?

Rachiah was more Ryland's type with her exotic looks and distrustful gaze at anything male. She was a spitfire, too.

Sherri was sweeter, not plainer but pretty in a different way, a simpler more natural way.

She was more Kyle's type. But how did he explain that to Ryland without making it into a game, a competition in their otherwise normal day-to-day? Because Ryland would grab onto any game and hold on tight, especially if he was competing against Kyle.

Kyle didn't respond besides a slight nod of his head. He wouldn't encourage Ryland. He wouldn't. He didn't want to engage in any type of competition with his cousins. They were too close a family for anything like that to come between them. Especially over a woman.

Cyan clung to Jareth's hand, her vulnerable softening visible only to those in the bridal party as she met Jareth's eyes and he led her to the officiator.

Her bouquet wasn't blue. Everything else seemed to be. But she'd gone with bright yellow sunflowers as big as a man's spread hand with deep black centers and green stalks that hung down two feet. The contrast was appealing and eye drawing.

Kyle couldn't be more excited for her to be his new sister. He scanned the crowd for Ruby – the little sister he hadn't seen in a few years. Would he recognize her? There were his parents. His mother dabbed at the corners of her eyes and their dad appeared vaguely ill, like maybe someone might ask him to work at any moment.

But no sign of Ruby.

She hadn't made it to her oldest brother's wedding?

Hopefully, that wasn't true. Hopefully, Kyle didn't have to go to northern Idaho to bring her home and straighten things out. He'd already spent the greater part of the last five years stalking Guy.

"You may now kiss the bride." The pastor folded his arms and waited.

Kyle shot his gaze to Sherri, their eyes locked and her cheeks flushed. Would she blush like that when she was kissed? She didn't seem shy at all.

Cyan and Jareth embraced.

Ryland leaned toward Kyle once again. "The chick I walked with called me a name." He knit his eyebrows together, his frown fleeting but there. "At least I think that's what she did. She said '*aw, frass*'. Is that what she was saying? Was she calling me a… well, you know."

Startled, Kyle's mouth opened an imperceptible amount and a small laugh that was barely above a whisper burst from him. He leaned over after a second and murmured, "No, frass is bug droppings. She pretty much said 'aw, crap'."

"Hmm. She's pretty interesting." Ryland studied Sherri as she watched Cyan and Jareth with her smaller bouquet of daisies pressed to her chest.

They all clapped and Kyle swallowed the jealousy building in his chest.

There was nothing to be jealous about. Ryland thought she was interesting. That's about as far as it would go. Ryland was even less about commitment than anyone else. Well, Kyle was about to say Jareth, but Jareth was getting married, so that comparison didn't help Kyle's argument in the slightest.

Sherri wasn't Kyle's. He did his job and protected her from Guy the night before. Anything extra was just that – extra. He didn't expect anything else from her, especially since he didn't know her.

He ignored the fact that he did know some things – like her pet tarantula, her penchant for bugs, and the fact that she cursed using scientifically correct terminology. All of that aside, Kyle could say he didn't know anything about her.

Too bad, those things just hinted at an extremely interesting woman with curves that went on for days.

Dang woman.

~~~

"Isn't Cyan beautiful?" Kyle's mom gushed over every detail of the wedding, running through the ceremony as if a narrator at a rodeo going over the previous events. "Did you see the way the flowers all matched the setting without actually matching? Very creative. I would love to plan a wedding that ended up looking like this." She folded her arms and smiled as she continued taking in the scene of the wedding guests milling about.

Kyle met his dad's gaze and lifted his eyebrows. His dad shrugged noncommittally and shoved his hands into his polyester pant pockets, bouncing slowly on the balls of his feet.

"Is Ruby not coming?" Kyle's bluntness overrode his instinct to stay away from touchy subjects. He didn't want to make things uncomfortable, but they never even mentioned his little sister like she didn't exist. Like she wasn't a missing part of the family.

There was enough age difference between Ruby and Jareth that she was rarely on his radar, but Kyle and she had been closer in age growing up and they'd been friends more so than brother and sister. He didn't like being the only one who seemed to miss her.

His mom averted her gaze. "An invitation was mailed. I'm not sure if she got it or not." She sipped the punch and watched the crowd milling in the cooling clouds of mist from the tops of the tents.

Growling, Kyle's dad wrapped an arm around his wife's shoulders. "We're going to get something to eat. Don't bring up *that* topic again."

The topic. Like his sister was to blame for Guy's horrible treatment of her. Like the victim was to blame. Like the shame was actually something the family bore. Righteous indignation shuddered through Kyle.

Kyle knew Ruby and she wasn't to blame for anything. He swallowed the bitter taste left in his mouth at the realization that his parents didn't see it that way. They still considered it an embarrassment on the family.

He couldn't remember the last family holiday she came to.

He bit the inner part of his cheek. There was nothing he could do to make them change their mind, but that didn't mean he had to stop looking for his sister or reaching out.

Out of the corner of his eye, Kyle caught a glimpse of Sherri slipping toward the bar set up by the house, moving from the busy bridal group in the midst of taking individual pictures.

Happy to change the focus on his attention, Kyle couldn't be more interested in what she was up to. He watched her, moving closer to snag the chance to talk to her.

A couple steps away, Kyle stopped abruptly. Ryland approached Sherri, his smile big and on target.

She turned to face Ryland and Kyle couldn't see her face, but he could see the delight in Ryland's as well as the way he reached out and tucked a strand of her hair into her braid.

No biggy. He could focus on Ruby's revenge, especially if he wasn't wrapped up in a woman like Sherri. If he got away from the wedding, he might be able to go stalk Guy that evening.

With mounting irritation adding to his energy, he needed to do something worthwhile. Watching from the sidelines while Ryland danced and flirted with Sherri wasn't something that would help him get over her or his jealousy.

If he was lucky, he'd get the chance to punch Guy that night. If not, maybe he'd take the chance to drink something stronger than Moose Drool.

Either way, he'd have to take Jareth's truck and have it back before they left the next morning for their honeymoon.

Fine. Or maybe he'd just go back to where they were staying and get some sleep. The last couple days had been exhausting.

One way or the other, he had to get Sherri from his mind. He'd never get back to normal, if Ryland ended up with her.

That thought didn't set well with Kyle. And he didn't want to focus too closely on why.

Chapter 7

Sherri

No matter how she tried catching Kyle's eye during the ceremony, only Ryland's gaze met hers. He was gorgeous as heck, but seemed more charming than she was into.

She wanted Kyle watching her. She didn't need to be saved at the moment and getting to know Kyle in a more neutral setting would be a better gauge on how much she was really attracted to him or not. He'd saved her. She didn't want to like him simply because he'd rescued her.

She, also, didn't want Ryland's blue eyes staring at her.

And it wasn't just at the ceremony. Everywhere she went during the reception, there Ryland was. Ryland at the bar. Ryland at the dance floor – even when she said she didn't want to dance.

Then a small weevil landed on the table beside her and she stared at the little guy, his long snout covering a very small goatee-style body part. Weevils were her favorite. They had so much personality and were like little old men with hipster tendencies. She smiled at the little guy about to reach out and pick him up.

Ryland sidled up to her table, saw the small bug and smashed its tiny exoskeleton under his thumb and wiped it on a napkin.

A weevil.

He'd smashed an innocent weevil for no reason.

Yeah, Ryland wasn't on her list of people she wanted to be around at the moment. Her breathing still hadn't returned to normal.

Kyle disappeared shortly after dinner was served, leaving Sherri with little to look forward to and his cousin to sit there and annoy her.

By the end of the night, Ryland's constant advances wore on her and she might have committed to a date later in the week.

She wouldn't admit it to anyone else, but even though he was persistent to the point of annoying, he was still persistent and *interested*. Sherri wasn't impervious to flattery.

She'd take it. Especially since the one she wanted to flirt with – no matter how clumsily – didn't seem available.

~~~

The working protocol for the department in that area was the same as in Billings. Sherri was debriefed quickly and rushed through the new-hire programs fast for familiarization purposes.

According to her new boss, Barry Fields, that particular field office had been short-staffed for quite a while and didn't have anyone on fieldwork. With the recent droughts spanning over the last couple years, they needed the research more than anything.

Sherri had smiled and gathered the equipment she needed to pile into the truck they gave her. They would catch her up on more procedures and introduce her to the community at a later date.

Out on the trail, she studied the needles of the western pines along the ridgeline just northeast of the reservation and Taylor Falls. Barry had mentioned severe drought and some of the ranchers at the wedding on Saturday had bemoaned the dry spring and summer months, wishing for a longer, wetter fall. Many had mentioned fire hazards and lost crops. Many of the same words that usually sent a thrill down Sherri's spine.

Fire. The biggest fear she had stemmed from a lost home due to a house fire spread from a forest fire when she was little. Nothing was more detrimental to wild life and people than an unchecked fire started by careless humans.

Pine needles strewn about the floor, loose bark from trees, even dry roots could all be great signs that there was danger of fire in the area. The best sign there was fire danger was to follow the drought line. Because where there was drought, there were western pine beetles – a terrific natural indicator of fire danger in the northwest.

Bull pine were usually the first to drop their needles when beetles were present. Along the tree line, the needles elicited the telltale yellowing at the edges. In trees that were named for their evergreen qualities, the yellowing wasn't an indication of season change, but rather an indication that Sherri's bug friends were in the area.

A healthy swarm of beetles could decimate an entire hillside of trees with the right conditions, making things worse than they already were.

Out on a trail along the ridgeline, Sherri knelt beside the nearest tree with a trunk spanning only ten inches in diameter. The bark had small yellow holes with a collection of frass and wood at the openings.

She peeled at pieces of the bark, the weak tree restricting its sap production due to the lessened water resources. Sap was the major line of defense for trees against predators like bugs. With no water available to create extra sap, trees had a weakened defense system.

She continued crouching, looking along the canopy line for a break in the green fading to yellow. About a hundred yards down the trail, red needles broke up the monotony of the sick trees.

A red tree and another red and another red. A line of sick trees ending in a line of dead ones.

Sherri turned, facing the other way. Down the trail the way she had come, many trees had yet to exhibit yellowing needles. She stopped at each tree along the path and caressed their trunks, studying for the bore holes and any signs of frass.

Closer to the trailhead, fewer and fewer boreholes presented themselves, but they were still prominent enough to suggest the beetles migrated along the trail and down into the valleys.

Pulling out her pocket-notebook, she jotted the information down that she needed and returned to the truck. Alerting nearby ranches would be the first step of protocol on her way back to the office to input warnings and official statements via her boss. She wouldn't go out of her way but there were a few ranches she passed to get out to the national forest that she could stop and warn.

The truck rumbled and bumped over the dirt road as she drove. The first ranch butting up to the national forest was Jonesy's Acres. The long rolling plains co-mingled with the sides of the mountains as they jutted out.

Billings had been a different type of beautiful, different shades of browns and greens. There, in Clearwater County, the greens had a vibrancy which challenged the depth of the blues of the skies and waters and the golds of the fields and sun.

Even while Sherri wanted to get out and explore the world, she was never happier than right there breathing in the crystal clean air from the Montana mountains.

Gravel crunched under her tires as she rolled up the long dirt drive to Jonesy's ranch house. With her window down, the heat passed by with a cooling blast. As soon as she stopped, the illusion of cooler days stopped and she scowled at the rising temperature.

The heat wouldn't help the forest fire potential. Neither was it a good sign that rain was coming. Always before a good storm, cool winds kicked up, sending a shiver along your spine. But that wasn't happening and Sherri resented the heat of the late summer.

From her seat in the truck, she looked around at the parking area at the end of the drive.

Near the barn doors, men passed by, riding on horseback while others bucked hay bales into the back of a large work truck.

She climbed from the company rig, dusting off her jeans and scanning for the foreman or the owner. The dust had settled from her arrival along the dirt packed edges of the driveway and she raised her hand to shade her eyes as she continued searching for someone to discuss the concerns with.

A tall cowboy on a tan Arabian horse galloped toward her. His face hid in the shadow of his cowboy hat. His broad shoulders leaned forward as he moved with the horse and approached Sherri.

As he came closer and his features came into view, Sherri's breath caught.

Kyle.

She had disappointedly thought she wouldn't see him again. The cool set to his features made her wish that was still the case. He didn't seem glad to see her or the fact that she was there. Maybe he'd left the wedding early because of her. He hadn't been interested and she'd been too cloying with her continual glances his way. Leave it to Sherri to run a guy off after he'd saved her.

He drew abreast of her and dismounted, a sheen of sweat gathering at his brow and his bandana damp at his neck. He reined his horse to the side and then back. "Sherri. Are you here to see Ryland? He's working until seven."

Confused, Sherri motioned toward the mountains. "Um, no. I mean, I didn't know you guys

119

worked here." She furrowed her brow. "Is the owner here or foreman maybe?"

Kyle tugged off his gloves and slapped them on his upper thigh, a puff of dust clouded around his rear. "I'm the acting foreman while Nate's with Emma. Jonesy is back east with family. There's been a death and he needed to be there to help resolve matters." He studied her, a hand on the pommel. "What can I do for you, Sherri?"

His formality was offsetting and after the overwhelming warmth from Ryland two days before, Kyle's coldness slapped her across the face.

Maybe he was a different man than the one who had stood in her kitchen with his shirt off and then in her bedroom close to screaming at a spider.

She shook her head to push the thoughts out. She had a job to do. She could be just as professional as he was. "There is serious western beetle infestation along the western ridge. There are no guarantees that there will be a fire, but if there is a cigarette dropped or any dry lightning storms, the chances are raised drastically for an all-consuming fire."

Sweeping her hand across the landscape, she peered at him. "The fields will be wiped out and on over that way toward the orchard. Is there a basic irrigation set up for fire prevention?"

"I believe so." His hat brim covered his eyes while he considered what she said. After a moment, he looked up, his mouth grim. "I'll pass along your information to Nate when he gets back. Is there anything else?"

Anger started to build as he dismissed her so readily. "Yes, this is on an official capacity. It will be noted in my report that the Jonesy Acres was warned about western pine beetle infestation and fire danger." She set her jaw and turned around, holding back any further biting comments.

"Wait, Sherri." His tone had softened and when she turned, so had his expression. He nodded. "Thanks, I'll pass it along. Nate might call you."

She didn't bother responding, still stung by his treatment. She hadn't done anything and she'd be hanged, if he thought he could work hot and cold on her like that.

Now she wanted to see Ryland, just for a moment to feel like someone thought she was worth talking to.

A handsome cowboy at that.

.

Chapter 8

Kyle

Kyle had been curt and hadn't meant to be. Why couldn't he be more like Nate, more purposeful, more intentional?

He waited until dinner that night to call Nate. "Hey, man, Land Management visited today." As far as Kyle was concerned, Nate didn't need to know more than that about who came out. Why would he care that the woman who'd visited just happened to drive Kyle to distraction? No one needed to know that. He continued, "The agent said there was pine beetle infestation along the western ridge. Something about fire danger and fire prevention and control."

He hadn't been able to stop staring at her in her khaki-colored button up shirt and dirt-stained jeans. She'd been a refreshing sight on that hot day.

"Western pine beetles? I'll be there tomorrow. That's serious stuff. Did they say how bad the infestation went?" Nate's tone turned urgent.

"No, but I said you might call her." Kyle should've written down the information or asked for a copy of a report.

"Call the office tomorrow and have the agent join us at the ranch. We need to narrow down exactly what the problem is and how we can prevent any damage." Nate's voice lowered. "I'll be able to come tomorrow, but the next day I need to take Emma to Seattle for some tests."

"Is the cancer back?" Kyle swallowed against the sick feeling in his chest. They needed Emma – not just Nate. All of the Montana Trail cousins did. She was their glue.

"We're not sure. I'll be there first thing." Nate's sigh cut off as he hung up.

If Kyle had to deal with half the heartache Nate did, he'd avoid discussing it, too.

Ryland pushed past Kyle to stand beside the wall and tapped his boot, staring at Kyle all the while.

Slowly hanging up the landline phone, Kyle watched Ryland while suspicion reared its head. "What do you need, Ryland?" He couldn't shake his irritation with his smooth-talking cousin, not since the wedding and Ryland's infatuation with Sherri.

Not since he'd driven Sherri away from Kyle.

Seeing Sherri that afternoon had only reinforced his irritation with Ryland. Why did the guy have to horn in on anything? On everything?

"I need to make a phone call." He lifted the receiver. "Say, we have Friday off this week, right? Or is it Thursday? I can never remember."

"Thursday." Kyle narrowed his eyes. Why did he want to know his days off? Ryland was like the rest of them and preferred working over anything else. In fact, on the nights Kyle disappeared to watch Guy, Ryland usually covered for him because he liked the work.

But Kyle kept his questions to himself and moved over to the table setup along the side wall as if he had something important to write down.

Ryland dialed and then spoke softly, his laughter the only thing carrying over the milieu of the rest of the ranch hands talking at the dinner table. Suddenly noticeable, a grandfather clock ticked and tocked with annoying loudness between Kyle and the phone.

Ryland's last words carried just fine though. "Sounds good. I'll see you Thursday at six." He hung up and whooped, slapping Kyle's back as he passed with a grin the width of the Big Sky plains.

Kyle's scowl deepened. He was seeing someone on Thursday night. Who? The suspicions left Kyle's chest tight and conflicted. What if it was Sherri? Why would she go with Ryland?

Why wouldn't she?

If Ryland had a date with Sherri, Kyle might break one of his rules about competing with family. Kyle saw her first. That should be the deciding factor.

Who did Ryland think he was anyway?

~~~

Kyle reined in the Arabian he borrowed from Jonesy. Nate waited for Kyle on the deck, sitting on the log pole seats set up around the perimeter for optimal viewing.

The ranch was well laid out and went as far back in Jonesy's family as some of the railroads in the state. Jonesy's family had actually made their money on the success of trains in the area. He came from old money and the sprawling nature of the house and lands had a more relaxed feel than what the owner expected from his workers. He'd left simply because he had no other choice and he'd heard great things about Nate and his cousins. At least, that's what he'd claimed before he'd left for the airport.

Dismounting, Kyle set the Arabian free in the fenced in pen until he had a chance to put her away. Adequately cooled off, she'd get her fill of water and oats at the side of the pen.

Climbing the steps, Kyle glanced down the drive, startled to find Sherri's work truck moving toward him. He didn't have long to prepare Nate for who exactly the agent was.

Joining Nate at the table, he thumbed toward Sherri. "You know this agent, Nate."

Distracted, Nate looked at Kyle but didn't seem to really *see* him. "Hmm?" His gaze shot past Kyle. "Sherri?" He stood, waiting for her to join them on the porch.

"Hi, Nate." She approached confidently, arms swinging and in one hand a clipboard. She pushed her soft curled hair back and smiled warmly.

Kyle would give anything to have her look like that at him again – even if it meant he had to face that spider of hers.

Nate waited until she took a seat and then claimed his. Kyle followed suit and stretched his legs out in front of him. He was there to understand what was going on and to carry out any decisions Nate made on how to manage the ranch. He wouldn't lie – at least to himself – that getting to watch Sherri made the time much more enjoyable.

"I'm sorry to hear about Jonesy's family. I don't know the man, but it must be fairly serious to pull him away during the busy season." Sherri sat forward, ignoring Kyle.

"Yes, well, as unfortunate as it has been for him, it has opened up an opportunity for the Montana Trails. We need experience in managing a ranch for our references. Now that we have this experience, we'll have more jobs open up to us." Nate leaned back as well, resting his arm on the edge of the small outdoor table. "What did you have to tell us, Sherri? I'm not fond of western pine beetles, but I have a feeling you know more which we need to learn."

Sherri's soft laugh and sympathy in her eyes made it hard for Kyle to look away. "Western pine beetles are my specialty. I'll keep it simple."

She flipped over a sheet of paper and produced a pen to sketch as she spoke. Her graceful hands swooped and slashed to enunciate each point. "Western pine beetles are a terrific indicator on the potential for forest fires and other devastating tragedies."

Drawing a line, she followed it with multiple lines like layers under the first and then simple tree trunks and roots beneath the first line. "If a tree doesn't have water for a long time, it goes into survival mode where everything it has is saved for basic survival. Nothing is expended for defense or offspring or anything other than the basics. A tree's best line of defense is its sap." She glanced at the men as if gauging their understanding. She must have seen something in their eyes that said they got it because she moved on.

"Okay, now let's say a tree's defenses are down and a western pine beetle decides to bore in. Nothing is going to stop that from happening. Usually this is just one or two trees, here and there. They pick the weakest ones. If they don't do it, then root rot or something else just as bad can get the tree from below and spread even to the healthier trees." She paused a moment, eyeing them.

"The important thing here isn't that the beetles are attacking the trees. They do that. They're very important to land and forest management. No, what we're noting here is the abundance of their attack. Many of the trees are weak. Which means it wouldn't take more than the slightest spark and the softest whisper of wind to roar into something epic." She tapped her pen on the table, the soft click enunciating the menace under her words.

"Wow, you don't hold anything back, do you?" Nate whistled low as he stared out over the ranch he could see from his vantage point.

Sherri cocked her head. "Would it make it easier for you? I know it would lessen the importance of what I'm trying to extoll which doesn't meet my objective." Her fervent manners intrigued Kyle.

He couldn't stop watching her, if he tried. Her now familiar scent of citrus reached him on the warm air. Kyle didn't know how much longer he could take it without commenting on her allure.

"What do you suggest?" Nate peered at her as he leaned over the table and folded his hands as he watched her intently.

"My suggestions follow protocol as outlined here." She slid across a sheet of paper from her clipboard. "I would hasten to add though that if you don't have adequate irrigation, then a water line won't work. You'll need a fire line – no flames – but more like a dug ditch that spans a good twenty feet or so cleared of all grass or other vegetation. Just a stretch of dirt that the fire will have a hard time crossing." She pressed her lips together, before continuing. "Stock a lot of sand or something, Nate. It's so dry, I'm not sure water would work as a fire deterrent anyway."

"Thank you, Sherri. We will take your suggestions into consideration. I'll contact Jonesy tonight." Nate smiled at Sherri.

"My pleasure. I'm on my way to a few more ranches to explain the report. If you need anything, here's my card with my own cell number on the back.

You can reach me day or night." She shot her gaze toward Kyle then back at Nate, her smile tight.

"Thank you." Nate walked her to her truck and Kyle watched her rear-end as she walked away.

That's twice she'd driven away from him.

Back with Kyle, Nate pointed along the north border of the land. "While I'm gone, you guys can get the fire line dug. Why don't you oversee that? Change everyone's days off by a day. That way we have extra time to accomplish it. There's supposed to be lightning next week. With our Montana weather, that could easily move to this week. I'd rather be prepared and not lose Jonesy's hard work and ours while he's gone."

Kyle couldn't agree more. And delivering the news to Ryland that he had to cancel his plans added a bounce to his step.

He'd do whatever it took to make sure Ryland didn't date Sherri. The change in schedule delighted Kyle to no end.

Maybe he'd have to set up something with Sherri before Ryland could reschedule. He knew the schedules were changed. Ryland didn't.

He fingered the business card with her number on it. Kyle had her permission to call day or night – she hadn't specified the reason. Okay, technically Nate had permission, but Kyle was over the ranch while Nate and Jareth were gone. Didn't that permission switch to Kyle by proxy?

He'd see Sherri before Ryland, or he'd let that spider of hers crawl all over him.

Besides, how would Ryland treat Sherri? He didn't have a gentlemanly bone in his body.

Kyle tucked Sherri's card in his back pocket. Nate didn't need it. Kyle would call after Nate left, maybe after lunch and set something up.

His heart thumped with extra zeal at the thought of spending time with her.

Hopefully she chose him over Ryland. Besides, didn't he have first dibs? He'd rescued her from Guy. Didn't that make him her knight or something?

Whatever gave him an edge, he'd take. What was the saying? All's fair in love and war.

Chapter 9

Sherri

Who did Kyle think he was? He had rescued Sherri from that snake at the bar – at least according to what Rachiah reported and according to his own report. But what nobody seemed to understand was Sherri didn't need saving. She could do it on her own.

She conveniently ignored the fact that she'd been drugged. She didn't need to be reminded of that. Ignore the details. It kept it convenient anyway.

Rachiah had shared a few details right before she'd left again for Wyoming. The search for her father needed to end soon. She was torn in too many directions and the pain in her heart affected her friends.

Whatever, none of it mattered. Kyle's charm and playfulness initially didn't overshadow his moodiness now. And Ryland's charm now wasn't enough to cover how uncomfortable Sherri had been with his opening frankness.

The two cousins were a conundrum that Sherri didn't have time to deal with at that point in time. Maybe after work she could figure out how to feel. But the beetle danger needed to be reported and she had dreaded paperwork to fill out.

She barreled toward the office in her rig, her radio crackling a couple times before she realized she was getting a call.

"Sherri, come in. Sherri."

She lifted the hand-piece to her mouth and pressed the button, slowing her speed. The trees and fields came into focus from the blurry scenery as she'd rushed toward the field office. "Sherri. Over." She let off the button and held the mouthpiece inches from her face as she waited for more.

"The Sherriff reported campers up on Beaver Ridge. Can you check it out? Your report suggests anything can be hazardous. They're enforcing the no camper rule. Over."

Campers. Great. Now Sherri had to go ruin their good time. Camping on a Tuesday didn't seem that fun to her. A forest fire was even less fun, though, so she' do it. "Of course. I'm nearby. I'll finish up ranch notifications afterward. Over." She replaced the radio piece and turned around on the empty dirt road.

All the paperwork and talking to people defeated her reasons for being in that field – mainly not having to deal with people and only being around insects. Hadn't the last visit with Kyle and Nate proven how inconsistent people could be?

She'd have to pass Jonesy's Acres on her way to the ridge. Kyle would probably think she was stalking him or something. Her eye twitched at that possibility.

In no time, she reached the trailhead. Another car parked at the lead parking spot with tinted windows hid any belongings or hints at the owners' whereabouts. Great. They really might be camping.

Sherri grabbed her hat, the ridiculous flat, wide-brim ones that resembled Canadian Mounties and slammed it on her head. Clicking the bag of essential items into place around her waist, she slid from the truck. Slathering on sunblock, she headed out with her stride long and her intentions purposeful.

After a good hour of hiking, Sherri wiped at her sweaty brow. There wasn't a living soul on that trail. The car was there – she'd checked a couple dozen times as she hiked the trodden path back and forth, looking for evidence of anyone off the trail where they shouldn't be.

She'd have to go further off-trail. The least safe option, but if the car was there, then people were out in the woods. The only option left to look was deeper in the forest. What exactly were the campers doing?

Would they go east or west? She plopped her hands on her hips and glanced around as if the bark on the trees would tell her where they'd gone and how many there were.

Zero hints left her completely in the dark. She closed her eyes a minute and just breathed in the air. A soft, cooler but not too cool undercurrent on the air pulled her toward the east. There would be less heat to the east.

To the west the trails were more difficult to maneuver and the sun would beat down harder on that side of the mountain at midday. Taking a deep breath, she lifted her shoulders and pulled them back. "East it is." She followed her mutterings with a puff of air up her face to try to find a way to cool off. She'd need to duck into the shadows anyway and climbing off trail would at least get her into the shade.

Hopefully, the campers were looking for *easier*, just like Sherri. She picked her way over fallen logs covered in moss and large rocks shiny with venous quartz. The shade dropped in temperature by a noticeable amount, giving Sherri room to breathe.

She sighed, removing her hat and fanning herself with the flat brim. Gusts of air chilled her damp skin. Oh, thank Heaven. Beautiful pine scents smothered the dust on the air, making it easier to breathe.

She hadn't planned on being out that long, only supposed to stop at a couple ranches and then head back to the office. She hadn't brought enough water either. She called in to the office with her radio. "Central, this is Sherri, come in. Over."

"Central, here. Sherri, you find the campers yet?" The gruff tones gave Barry away as the operator. He must have stepped in to cover for lunch or something.

"No campers in sight. Car is here, but no campers on the trail. Heading off trail to the east. I will radio in thirty, if I haven't found them. Over." She really shouldn't leave the trail alone, but they didn't have enough personnel for her to wait for someone to join her.

Plus, the sooner she found those hikers, the sooner she could get out of there.

"Be careful. Over." His disapproval was palpable, but what could he do? Sherri needed to warn those campers and she was taking precautions to stay safe.

She retucked the radio to her hip and continued down the hill, spotting the Jonesy ranch through the descending tree line. Just what she didn't need, a reminder that Kyle was as close as he was.

Just catching a glimpse of Kyle or Ryland didn't seem like it would be in her best interest. She narrowed her eyes as she stepped carefully around roots protruding from the loose dirt and ducked under branches stretching for her obnoxious hat.

She made it half-way down the hillside before coming to a stop at the sight of a horse carrying Kyle came toward her.

Of course, it did. Of course, when she was sweaty and a mess and out of breath and dehydrated, there he would be. Like the flies she continued batting at. She liked bugs but not when they pointed out how much she smelled.

Dang it all, she didn't need saving. How many times would he find her in situations where he would think she needed to be saved? She didn't need help from anyone. She was fine.

She stopped beside a tree and pulled off her hat again, fanning herself and catching her breath. Sherri nodded as he got closer, a tight smile all she could bring herself to offer.

He pulled the horse to a stop when he reached a spot with a slight plateau in it. He slid from the horse, his stacked jeans not sliding above his boots. Glancing around the woods and then down at the fence along the property line, he held onto the reins in one hand while setting his other on his belt line. Tilting his head toward her, he studied Sherri's form before asking, "You okay?"

"Of course. Why wouldn't I be?" She forced her breaths to come longer and slower. She didn't need to pass out in front of him. She was definitely not one for exercising and that had never been more apparent than when she was standing there feeling like she might die of embarrassment in front of the extremely delicious cowboy that drove her insane with his nearness.

Kyle eyed her, pulling a canteen that hung from a leather strap around his neck. "Here, it's hot out here. Why are you out this far? I just sent Damon with two hikers back up to their car. They got lost or something. They weren't prepared either. No water. Nothing to keep the sun off their necks, nothing."

The judgement in his tone rankled. "I'm prepared. I just wasn't *as* prepared as I would have liked. My boss asked me to do a job that hadn't been on my worksheet this morning." Sherri bit back more irritation and allowed the relief to well in her gut. "I'm glad you found them. I was out here to warn them not to light any fires or drop cigarettes or anything." The bark of the tree behind her bit into her back as she leaned her shoulders against it, even through multiple layers of her bra and two shirts.

"It's that serious, huh?" He tucked his thumbs into his front pockets and watched her with a more relaxed demeanor than the last few times she'd talked with him. The auburn of his hair peeked beneath the low-slung brim of his hat.

She warmed to her topic, seeking to focus on anything but the way the cowboy filled his jeans just right. "Oh, yes, the Western Pine Beetle is the smartest indicator we can use to help warn us of potential fire. It would be terrible to lose anything because we failed to acknowledge quasi-predicting elements." She pushed her hair off her forehead, puffing cool air over her face.

The heat wasn't letting up, even in the shade. Sherri still had to get up the mountain to get to her truck. She half-turned, glancing back the way she'd come and wincing at how far it actually looked.

"Come on. I'll give you a ride up to your truck." Kyle held out his hand to help her up onto the saddle. There didn't seem to be any judgement in his eyes, but she didn't know him well enough to tell for sure.

"Really?" She looked around like maybe the drying ferns and yellowing needles would tell her she was in a dream. Walking down had been horrible, she didn't want to go up at all. She gulped at the cool water in his canteen, cautious not to overdrink. She should leave him something. As much as she wanted to keep her pride wrapped around her, she wanted even more to not have to climb that mountain in her uncomfortably hot work clothes. She cleared her throat and nodded tightly. "Okay, yeah, thank you." She eyed him, then the horse. "Can I ride behind, though?"

Startled, he studied her for a moment, and then nodded. "That's fine with me."

She didn't need to sit in front of him, just under his nose without knowing if she stank or not. He was still good looking as sin and she didn't want to take the chance he'd not only find her nerdy but completely unattractive as well. She'd studied dung beetles, that didn't mean she wanted to smell like one.

He mounted the Arabian, offering his hand again but to help her up behind him.

She clumsily climbed onto the rump of the horse and wrapped her arms around Kyle's solid waist. The thought crossed her mind to press her cheek to his back where his broad shoulders offered stability and strength, but her common sense stopped her in time.

The loping of the horse pushed her against him and heat flooded her cheeks from more than the sun. She leaned as far back as she could, her hat clutched in her hands. She couldn't bring herself to put the sweaty sticky thing back on. Her head needed to breathe. At least for a little longer.

"So, um, do you have anything going on Friday night?" His chest vibrated down to his sides and under her hands as he spoke.

She looked at the back of his neck under his hat brim like she could read his mind or something. Was he asking her out? Sherri shrugged. "Nothing, probably. I need to feed my tarantula but that's about it."

"Really? I bet that's cool." He didn't turn, so he couldn't see her expression of astonishment.

Branches grazed their legs as they passed, the pace sedate. Sherri could actually look around at the setting instead of worrying about where she was stepping or if her next footfall would be her last.

She wrinkled her nose and replied, "Yeah, I guess." What did he want? He'd been terrified of the spider walking on his shirt when he'd been over. Why would he think watching it eat would be interesting?

He leaned forward over the horse's neck as it climbed up a little bit steeper point and spoke as if an afterthought. "Well, maybe I could pick up some dinner and come help. I noticed you had boxes packed at your place. I could help you unpack. I'm good with heavy stuff."

Shocked didn't do her reaction justice. She opened and closed her mouth a few times. Ryland was taking her out Thursday and now Kyle wanted to go out with her? No, he wanted to come to her place and help her with her spider and boxes?

What was going on? She never had dates, let alone delicious cousins who just happened to be

151

cowboys. Had she fallen into some opposite dimension? If so, maybe she never needed to leave.

Shaking her head in disbelief, she nodded, slightly. Wasn't he the one she wanted to go out with? Wasn't he the one she was interested in? Ryland was more like a balm on her ego when it seemed like Kyle wanted nothing to do with her.

He spoke before Sherri could answer. "I understand if not. I just thought we could hang out." The reins in his hands didn't move as he maneuvered the beautiful horse up the incline.

"Yeah, that sounds good. I'm a vegetarian though." She ignored the tightening of his chest when he registered what she'd said.

"Really? As in no meat?" He turned his head to see her from the side, curiosity instead of judgment on his chiseled features.

She shook her head with a smile. "I know, it's weird up here, but I'm not a fan of eating meat. I'll do dairy and even fish, so I guess I'm really a pescatarian, but vegetarian is easier for people to get. Is that a problem?" For some reason, his answer mattered. If he said yes, what then? Would she take it personally? Why would he care what she ate?

He drew the horse onto the more level trail and evened out into a comfortable pace. "Not at all. I'll bring something for both of us to enjoy."

They reached her truck in minutes. The other car gone from the parking area.

Kyle helped Sherri dismount the horse and he followed, moving to stand beside her rig while she unlocked the door.

She should get back to the office, but she suddenly didn't want to get out of there as fast as she had before. She pulled on the handle, opening the door about an inch, unsure what to say or what to do.

Kyle placed a hand on the frame of the driver door and stopped her from opening it fully. His husky low voice sent chills along her skin, out of place for the warm summer heat. "I like you, Sherri. I hope to

153

get to know you better." The tender way he said it and the sudden ruddiness to his skin gave away his embarrassment and discomfort.

And by Jove, Sherri's jaw dropped. What in Sam's hades was going on? Was it a competition or something between the cousins? Why else would two gorgeous men like Kyle and Ryland ask her out?

She snapped her mouth shut and nodded shortly. "I'm looking forward to it, too." Great, now she sounded as formal as she could get. Why couldn't she have said something similar to what he'd said? She liked him. At least, she liked when she was around him and seemed like the guy standing in her kitchen that morning.

He tilted his hat at her, remounting the horse and riding off at a slight amble.

Sherri didn't know how to date one guy and then another. Were they going to talk about their dates with her? Compare notes? She wasn't designed for multiple boyfriends. Heck, she'd never had the problem of more than one guy liking her and he didn't count since he was pretty much her brother.

She'd have to call Rachiah and see what she thought. If anyone could wrap a handful of men around her finger and make them like it, it was her.

Nerves clanging, Sherri realized she wasn't sure just what to do and that alarmed her. She wasn't prepared for the situation.

Plus, Kyle wanted to go to her place to feed the tarantula. He'd been upset when he'd seen Tommy out. Maybe she should tease him and ask him if he was going to cry when she took Tommy out to feed him. She didn't want to make a grown man cry.

But stranger things had happened.

And just what did Ryland want to do? He had no idea about her fascination with insect life. Would he be as comfortable with it as Kyle seemed to be?

~~~

Nate

Nate couldn't contain his anxiety. His left leg jiggled as he pressed on the gas and the brake with his right. There was too much uncertainty in his life right then. Emma was… getting sick but she didn't want to go into the doctor.

He'd finally convinced her to go and things weren't looking good.

After a slew of tests, he'd had to go back to the Jonesy ranch. But headed back to be with Emma, he couldn't wait to hear the results of the tests. He needed to know what was wrong with his wife. They hadn't had long together, yet. Not long enough. He needed longer.

Plus… Emma was getting more depressed. Not because she was tired or not feeling well. Hannah had pulled him aside and told him that Emma had seen a

Mrs. Hamsling at the store with her newborn baby boy and started crying.

Emma crying in public was impossible, but Hannah assured him it had happened. She'd mentioned before how sorry she was that they couldn't have babies. How many times had Nate tried to tell her that she was enough for him? Just her. She was all he needed.

But… maybe she needed more. Emma needed more than Nate and there was nothing he could do to give that to her.

And that tore him apart.

He could work and work and work, but that would never give her a baby that she wanted. There was nothing to be done for that.

His phone buzzed. Putting the speakerphone on, he held the phone in one hand facing him while watching the road. "Yeah."

"Nate? Are you coming back?" Emma's weak voice made him push harder on the gas. "I'm… The doctor is supposed to come in and tell me my results in a couple hours. Will you be here?" Her words ended on a rasp as she trailed off.

Tightening his hold on the steering wheel, Nate nodded at no one in particular. "I'm coming, honey. I'll be there soon." He had a couple hours left, but he swore on all that was within his power and then some that he'd beat the doctors getting to her room.

He would. He had to be there for her. She was his everything. She needed him. Just like he needed her.

Chapter 10

Kyle

Steak was pretty much the only meat or main entrée Kyle was familiar with. Sherri and her vegetarian thing had thrown him for a loop. Seafood seemed to be a go-ahead, but in the middle of Montana, what did that mean?

Kyle had all week to worry about his food choice for Friday. Every time he passed Ryland he couldn't help smiling smugly at his cousin.

Until Thursday night when Ryland disappeared right after their late shift – about eight.

Ryland didn't get back to the bunk until well after one in the morning.

Kyle was certain of the time because he paced by the clock in the bunk kitchenette well past midnight. He'd memorized the size and shape of the floor pattern as well as the annoying pause in every fifth tick of the second hand on the clock. Ryland had disappeared to his bunk without a word, leaving Kyle even more uncertain of what was going on.

The next morning, Kyle watched Ryland whistle his way through the breakfast line and claim a seat across from Kyle to eat.

Drinking half his coffee, Kyle ignored the burning sting as it coursed down his throat. When he spoke, an extra hoarseness coarsened his words. "You were out late last night." That was nothing like what he wanted to ask. No, he wanted to wrap his fingers around Ryland's neck and shake him until he got every last word about the night before out of his annoyingly charming mouth.

Eyes sparkling with amusement, Ryland looked up from the hashbrowns he shook salt on. "What are you, my mother?"

How did Kyle respond? He couldn't necessarily press for more information – at least not without sounding like, well, like Ryland suggested – his mother. At the same time, he had to know what he was up against.

Instead of pushing like he longed to, Kyle shrugged, picking at his plate with his fork. He didn't even care what was on it. He shrugged, grinning like he didn't really care, even though he did. Desperately. "Nah, I'm just curious."

As if he was part of the conversation, Damon leaned over his plate, poking into the air with his rolled-up pancake. "I bet you were out with that girl, what's her name?"

Ryland grinned, leaning back and drinking his orange juice. "Don't worry about it, guys. I had fun last night. That's all you need to know." He winked and glanced around at the rest of the small hall area. "Hey, where's Nate?"

Their joviality faded. Ryland sat forward, leaning his forearms on the table edge. He played with the whorls in the plate pattern with the handle of his knife. "From what I learned last night; Emma isn't doing well. She's extremely tired and can't stand for more than a few minutes at a time. Nate has her at a hospital in Seattle by her parents to get some testing done, but they're not sure what to hope for. He was supposed to hear yesterday or today."

"Maybe she's pregnant." Damon opened his hand, putting a positive spin on Emma's plight.

A different outcome that would be great for everyone was exactly what Kyle needed to hear. He slapped the table. "Yeah, maybe she's pregnant. That'd be great." He grinned, grateful to have something else to focus on. Thinking about Ryland and Sherri wasn't starting his day off the right way.

"Would it? I don't think she can because of all the radiation and stuff she had growing up, but maybe." Ryland shrugged, pasting a smile over his worry.

How did Ryland know all those facts? Had he been spending more time with Nate? Not possible with Nate in Seattle. He would have to hang out with someone closer to the picture. Would that nameless person be Sherri?

More than concern over Emma's health ate at Kyle's gut.

Nerves over his date that night welled inside him. Excitement had overridden anything anxious until right then. The possibility that Ryland had spent time with her the night before, despite Kyle's best efforts to ruin those plans, didn't sit well with him.

What if she dated both of them and decided Kyle wasn't… Kyle shook his head. *Wait, just wait. Don't go getting ahead of yourself.*

"What are you so serious about?" Ryland scowled at Kyle; his previous good humor faded at the conversation about Emma.

Kyle frowned. "Emma. I want her to be safe." *And I want Sherri off your radar.* But he shoved a bite of peppers and sausage into his mouth before his desire to speak his mind overrode his instincts to keep his opinions to himself.

Plus, if he let Ryland know just how much Sherri meant to Kyle, Ryland would do everything he could to get in the way. Just to prove he could.

Ryland polished off the rest of his breakfast and stood, clearing his plate. "You have today off, right, Kyle? Is Jareth taking over?" He paused beside Kyle, looking down at him.

"No, Jareth is still on his honeymoon. I was going to ask if you'd mind covering for me." Kyle wasn't really planning on that, but maybe giving Ryland some responsibility would be a good way to keep him in hand.

Ryland scoffed. "Yeah, 'cause I'm the first choice of everyone to lead the group, right?" He narrowed his gaze at Kyle. "What are you up to, Darby?"

"Nothing. I'm off to find the best seafood I can in this area." He nodded, standing himself. "That's all I want to do today. Any suggestions?" He met Ryland's gaze and then glanced around at the rest of his cousins as well as a couple stray ranch hands who were more permanent fixtures at Jonesy's Acres but weren't quite old enough to take on a job like foreman.

Damon called out after him. "Rocky Mountain oysters. Get those."

Kyle ignored the men's laughter as it followed him from the room. The Johnson brothers could sometimes be more trouble than they were worth. But

Rocky Mountain oysters... maybe they were some kind of fresh water mussel or something. He was willing to try anything to impress Sherri. He had to standout over Ryland. His pride demanded it.

High-tailing it out of the ranch before he was snagged to solve a problem and potentially end up working for the day, Kyle rumbled into Taylor Falls in Jareth's old brown Ford. Usually on a ranch, Kyle didn't need a vehicle, he just chose to stay on premise and work hard or ride horses. Nothing calmed him faster or longer than just enjoying the God-given world he lived in.

He climbed out of the rig after parking and approached the small-town store. He had somewhere to start with what he was looking for.

The woman at the grocery counter looked at him kind of odd when he requested two pounds of Rocky Mountain oysters, but she wrapped them up and gave him strict instructions on how to cook them. Thank goodness for that, because he had no idea what he was doing. He couldn't get over the fact that there weren't any shells. Who knew there were mussels out there without a shell?

He picked up a Caesar salad kit – Sherri should be able to eat that with the anchovies in the dressing. He hoped so, anyway.

As he approached the door, the woman at the counter called out to him. "Did you get a sauce for the oysters?" He shook his head and she pointed toward the aisle closest to him. "Grab the sriracha, it has a nice heat but won't ruin the experience."

Kyle grabbed the first bottle he came across and approached the counter again, but half-way there she waved him on. "It's on me. You have an interesting night ahead of you." She winked and pointed at the bag in his hand. "Those are supposed to be great aphrodisiacs."

He blushed and nodded his head, mumbling his thanks as he ducked out the door.

An aphrodisiac. He didn't want Sherri to think he expected anything physical from her. Especially not on their first date. She had an innocence about her that reminded him of Ruby which made him want to protect her. Something about the set in her shoulders suggested she didn't want to be saved by anyone. Either way, she didn't deserve to be thought of like a piece of tail.

The fact that Guy had treated her like that when Kyle couldn't see her as anything but a person with value really irked him. He viewed her that way because she was.

At the entrance to the reservation, Kyle pulled over.

He needed a minute to gather himself.

Had Sherri been with Ryland the night before? Ryland was a smooth operator and usually charmed his way into second and third base with the girls he chased after. He wasn't the type of man who strutted either. If he got more than that, he never bragged about it.

In fact, the more Kyle thought about it, none of the Montana Trail cousins kissed and talked about it. Pride welled in his chest. At least they had *some* class.

He hung his head and breathed deep. Crap, why was he so dang nervous?

A rap of something metal on his window jerked his head upright.

M.T. stared at him through the glass, his eyebrow cocked. The feather in his hair was more ominous with its black shiny contours and long tip. He wore a loose tank top that displayed molded muscles even Kyle had to admit were a bit intimidating.

Kyle hadn't even considered that he might be doing something he shouldn't. He rolled down the window and smiled. "How goes it, M.T.?"

"It'd be going fine, if you'd tell me why you're parked in front of the lodge. Truck problems or something?" M.T. eyed the truck like he wouldn't be surprised, if the jalopy had broken down. "I can give you a ride into town. I'm supposed to run to the nursery and get some ladybugs for the aphids on my mother's pear trees."

"I'm, well, I'm heading in to see Sherri. I promised her dinner as a thanks for helping with a… uh, a bug problem at the Jonesy ranch. Make sure she's doing okay since that guy bothered her. Honestly, that incident left me a little antsy about her being out and about on her own." Why was he lying?

Well, not lying, more like stretching the truth, but something to the glint in M.T.'s dark eyes told him to keep it sounding platonic. Sounding simpler than it was.

But most likely simpler would be best.

"Checking on her is a good idea. I don't think Rachiah is around right now. Sherri is working hard, though. I'm not sure she should be busy all night." M.T. glared. "Sherri's great. Why don't you get along then? I'll stop by her place later to make sure she's alright. I'd rather not see you there." In other words, be gone.

Not that M.T.'s bluntness could be taken as subtlety on any level.

Kyle nodded, the brim of his hat chopping through his vision of M.T. and then returning him back to normal. "Well, like I said, it's just a thank-you dinner. You're welcome to join us." He lifted the brown bag from the seat beside him. "We're having Rocky Mountain oysters. I hear they're delicious."

Furrowing his brow, M.T. shot his gaze from the bag to Kyle's face to the bag and back. He chose not to reply but walked to his own truck with slow, steady strides. His broad shoulders enhanced the thickness to his biceps and Kyle was just secure enough to accept that the man's muscles were daunting and more than capable of pulverizing Kyle's bones. Kyle wasn't a wimp, but next to Maverick Two-Claw he didn't hold a candle in the size department.

What was with M.T.'s protectiveness? Did he have a thing for Sherri? If he did, then Kyle was playing with fire and he had no way to stop himself.

Kyle shifted the truck into drive and crept into the residential area of the reservation. Like the burning haze of a laser, Kyle could have sworn M.T.'s gaze bore into the back of his neck as Kyle drove.

Reaching the little cabin, Kyle breathed deeply in relief. But her little truck wasn't there and he really didn't want to be caught by M.T. like Kyle was lurking or something.

He shut off the truck's engine and climbed from the cab, grabbing the items he'd brought for dinner. If he had to, he'd wait in the small fenced-in backyard. He knocked on the door, glancing behind him like the Redhawk gang watched him from behind the trees or the lilac bushes on the corner of the street.

No answer and no noise from inside. He couldn't return to the truck. He couldn't take that chance. He tried the knob, even though what single girl wouldn't lock her door, right?

But the knob turned and the door swung open with little provocation. Kyle sighed in relief. He'd rather get caught by Sherri inside than by M.T. outside.

Besides, he could prepare the meal while he waited for her to show up.

He had some frying to do.

~~~

The Rocky Mountain oysters weren't easy to flour, especially when all Sherri seemed to have in her house was cornmeal, organic eggs, and some kind of almond milk that looked like white-colored water.

Kyle was a little nervous to touch the white block of stuff labeled tofu. He'd heard of it, but he'd never actually seen it, like a vague myth that just didn't seem to exist in the mountains of Montana.

She only had olive oil and some kind of coconut milk. Her pans were ceramic lined. Kyle searched the small house for some kind of cast iron or stainless steel. Something he wouldn't break or scratch.

He heated up a tablespoon of oil and prepared the oysters according to the instructions – or at least as much as he could remember from the woman at the store. Improvising with corn meal when the woman had said flour, he wasn't sure how much he was messing up.

Tossing the salad, he plated the freshly fried oysters and put them in the oven to keep warm. Then he sat down at the table and waited.

And waited.

Five-thirty came and went.

Five-forty-five gone after excruciatingly slowness.

Five-fifty-nine.

Six.

Where was she?

He double-checked the bedroom where the spider was to make sure the arachnid was contained. Kyle paced, he stared at the digital green clock on the microwave.

Finally, the sound of a car door shutting reached him and he stood, gazing toward the ceiling with its already recognizable swirls in the texturing.

She walked inside, digging in her bag. She looked up, scanning the room with her gaze. Her eyes lit on Kyle and she dropped her bag, shrieking. She drew out a canister of pepper spray and pointed it toward Kyle, her hand shaking.

He held up his hands. "Whoa, Sherri, it's me. You're okay. We had a date tonight, remember?"

She looked around again, her eyes wide. "We did? Tonight?" After a moment, she nodded slowly. Her hair moved softly against her shoulder. "Oh, that's right. Sorry, it's been a long week. People don't care about beetles half as much as they should." She sighed, rubbing her eyes. "I'm sorry…" She looked up, raising the pepper spray once again. "Wait, why are you in here? Why didn't you just leave and what is burning?"

She rushed around the counter in the kitchen and opened the oven door, releasing a cloud of smoke.

Kyle slapped his leg. "Dang it. I'm sorry. You wanted seafood. I brought Rocky Mountain oysters. I'd fried them and then put them in the oven to keep warm. I think they were in there too long."

Sherri placed the pan on top of the stove and closed it, a peculiar look on her face. She flipped off the controls and straightened, thrusting her hands on her hips. "I'm sorry, what did you say you made?"

Kyle swallowed, tucking his hands in his jeans pockets. "I made Caesar salad and Rocky Mountain oysters. You said you eat seafood. Or do you only eat fish?" All the rules were so complicated. Why couldn't she eat meat? He didn't care if they had peanut butter and jelly sandwiches to be honest. He really just wanted to spend time with her. Now they only had salad to eat.

She watched him, like she couldn't figure something out. Then she walked to the living room and flopped to the couch. She rubbed her eyes again and pointed at a spot beside her. She didn't speak until he sat. "Thank you so much for cooking for me. It's a little... creepy that you came in my home but I'm too tired to be mad."

He cut in. "I'm sorry, but M.T.—"

She held up her hand. "You could've left, Kyle." She sighed. "You're not going to convert me to eating meat. I was serious when I said I don't eat beef."

"I know." He knit his eyebrows. "I went to all that trouble to find that seafood and make it for you." His shoulders sagged. "I'm sorry I just came in. Looking back, sure, not such a bright idea. I really just wanted to see you and spend some time with you. Figure out why I can't get you out of my head or better yet, find out how to get you *out* of my thoughts. You're highly distracting, you know?"

"Is this a joke? Are you making fun of me?" She stood, moving in front of him with a stuttered pacing. "I don't think it's funny. M.T. protects me for a reason. He always has. And now, like in these types of instances, I can see how important his protection has been."

"Hey." Kyle shoved himself from the couch and grabbed Sherri's shoulders, pulling her to a stop and facing him. "What are you talking about? I protected you the other night. You're safe with me." He rubbed his thumb across her chin. "You're safe."

She jerked her face from his grasp. "They why would you make fun of my eating by trying to make me beef testicles?"

Blinking, Kyle dropped his hands and stepped back. "What?"

"You cooked cow balls, Kyle." She pointed into the kitchen, her eyes glinting. "When I say I don't eat cow, I'm serious. That doesn't mean I want to eat their private parts." Her eyes grew sad. "I really liked you, but now… you're just like the other guys."

"Wait. I'm seriously confused. I thought they were fresh water mussels. You're serious, I cooked testicles?" He swallowed, his mouth suddenly dry, his stomach queasy at the thought. "The guys… they…" Realization dawned on him with a slow fade. "I'm going to *kill* them."

Of course, they would make sure he looked like an idiot.

Uncertainty darkened her eyes and she frowned. "You didn't know what they were?"

179

Kyle moved closer, gently pushing her hair behind her neck. "I promise, I don't want to eat nuts. I certainly don't want to fondle them and bread them and then throw them in the fryer. I am, however, considering the possibility of neutering my cousins."

She stared at him, her anger fading and curling her lips into amused humor. "Really? You didn't know that's what they were? I thought you were raised in Montana." She shook her head, her eyes shutting for a brief moment.

"Who told you that?" Kyle cocked his head, his own humor derisive but good-natured.

She blushed. "I asked around about you. A little. Maybe." Her mumble warmed him. Shadows under her eyes testified to just how tired she was. What was it that she did that would exhaust her like that?

"I burned our dinner." He pressed his lips together. "Want to go out instead?"

She scrunched her lips in the cutest shape, twisting her nose at the same time. "I really have had a long day. I have some tofu we could have with the salad?" She smiled at his ill-concealed grimace. "And I think Rachiah left a steak in the freezer."

He brightened. "Really? A steak? You wouldn't be… mad at me for eating meat?" He could replace it the first chance

Her laugh warmed him and his worries faded. "Of course not. I'm the one who doesn't like meat. I wear a bra, too, but that doesn't mean I'm going to make you wear one." She cocked her eyebrow. "Unless of course you want to." She giggled.

"That sounds good. Not the bra, but the steak." He offered her his hand. "Let's go get dinner made."

She smiled, the bottom swell of her lips entrancing. "Sounds good, but I have no idea how I'm going to explain eating dinner with the guy who broke into my house." She winked. "Guess I'll tell Rachiah you broke in to steal her steak."

Her teasing shifted something inside him and he couldn't help it. He tugged her close and leaned in, his lips inches from hers. "How about I steal a kiss instead?" He bent his head before she could answer and their lips met, the moment stunningly sweet and poignant without any anxious planning.

She didn't pull away, sinking against his chest instead and warming to the simple contact that swelled in Kyle's chest with heat.

They broke away, a new appreciation for the other in their expressions. She didn't seem to think twice about reaching out and taking his hand again, like a natural habit they'd had for years. She laughed as they walked toward the kitchen, shaking her head. "Cow balls."

How lucky was he? He didn't have to eat cow testicles *or* tofu. He got to have steak with a woman he couldn't keep his mind off of.

Kyle's night was looking up.

Chapter 11

Sherri

Sherri laughed. In fact, she hadn't stopped laughing with Kyle since the Rocky Mountain oyster incident earlier that evening. When they'd dropped their shields, she couldn't believe how comfortable she was with him.

"Wait, I have one. Stop me, if you've heard this one." Sherri sipped her water to rinse the parmesan bits from her mouth and then met Kyle's expectant gaze. "If you have to choose between a big weevil and a small weevil—"

"A weevil? Like one of those bugs you find in flour?" Kyle arched his brow and leaned forward, confusion shadowing the gorgeous blue of his eyes.

Sherri nodded, snickering. "Yes, those ones."

"Go on." He nodded, waiting.

"If you have to choose, then choose the lesser of two weevils." She snorted at the end of the tagline. It was her favorite joke and she never got to tell it outside of the entomologist field because most people didn't care enough to hear it.

The joke was Kyle's test. Ryland had already failed the first one when he'd killed the weevil in front of her. Now, Kyle had a chance to prove he could handle just how silly she could be.

He leaned back, amazement on his face. "That was adorable." He chuckled. "Lesser of two evils. I get it."

His smile warmed her and she opened her mouth to comment but a knock on the door interrupted her.

After nine-o-clock who would be calling at her place? She stood. "Excuse me."

At the door, M.T. craned his neck when she opened the door to see inside. He spoke in low concerned tones. "That… ranch hand is still here. Do you want me to remove him? Is he causing problems?"

Irritation at being babysat edged her words a little sharper than she intended. "No. M.T. I'm fine. He's fine. It's fine. Thank you." She didn't want to be rude, but Maverick didn't have to show up and ruin her night. His actions were making her reconsider her decision to stay on reservation with Rachiah.

M.T. narrowed his eyes. "Fine." He turned away then turned back, stepping closer to Sherri. He took her hand in his and laced his fingers with hers, imploring her with his deep dark brown gaze. He spoke softly but earnestly as he look down at her from his tall height. "Sherri, don't pick someone like him. He's transient. He's not loyal. Pick me. Please, pick me. Give me a chance."

It always came back to him wanting her to pick him. Always. But he had no idea that she wasn't an option for him. Sherri had already been told the rules by Rachiah a long time ago.

Maverick was as close to pure blood Salish as you could get. He had expectations and Sherri would never be welcomed in.

As much as she loved M.T. as a friend, they would never fit together the way she wanted to fit with someone. And constantly having to tell Maverick they weren't right for each other wore on her nerves and her heart. Why did she have to hurt him?

Tears pricked at Sherri's tired eyes. She softly shook her head. "I'm not picking anyone tonight, M.T. I'm sending you both home so I can get some sleep. Goodnight." She retracted her fingers slowly, sad that his touch didn't make her wish they were locked up together alone in a cave instead of miles apart like they belonged.

She gently closed the door and turned to find Kyle standing close by. Sherri motioned over her shoulder feebly and with what had to be a shaky smile. "Sorry, long story."

Kyle moved closer, bending his head to meet her lowered gaze. "Nah, he cares for you. That's as long as it needs to be." He straightened up and smiled. "Well, your new nickname is Weevils." He playfully chucked her under the chin which turned into a caress of her neck, sending delicious shivers along her collar bones and down to her hips. "I better go. It's getting late and I have work to do tomorrow. Are you off?"

She nodded, still captivated by the lingering traces of his touch. "I don't have to work, but Ryland asked me to stop by the ranch, so maybe I'll see you?" Her hope felt like it glowed out of her with a huge warmth.

Kyle lurched backwards, dropping his hand from her arm. He blinked at her, his astonishment strong in the angles of his jaw and the widening of his eyes. "You're seeing him, too?"

"Too?" Sherri settled on her hip, thrusting a hand on the outer bent curve. "Who else am I seeing?" She wanted to date Kyle but they'd just gotten together that night and it hadn't exactly started conventionally. His hot and cold moods were getting on her nerves as well.

He tightened his jaw and stepped around her to claim the hat he'd hung from a hook by the door. "I thought you and I..." He shook his head. "I was feeling pretty cynical of M.T., thinking he needed to get the hint, but now I can't help wondering if maybe I should feel bad for any poor sucker interested in you. You're stringing a few of us a long." He pulled open the door, avoiding her gaze.

Sherri didn't reply. Instead, as soon as his foot cleared the doorway, she slammed the heavy wood panel shut. Turning to lean against it, she closed her eyes. Her week of warning so many ranches and dealing with sexism in her field had taken its toll. Combine her exhaustion with the little drama Kyle and M.T. had to dish up, and she was going to sink into a bathtub with a glass of wine.

Wine she didn't have.

She didn't even have chocolate – not that she would've had it.

But she'd give anything for a cheesecake. Something not so sweet, but creamy. How sad that a fun night had ended so harshly.

Bugs. Bugs had her back and didn't hurt. Men were like fire – they burned and destroyed everything in their path. Even the balls they cooked you for dinner. She shook her head and ignored the table.

Tomorrow. She could deal with stuff tomorrow.

Tonight.

Bath. And Tommy time.

~~~

If she hadn't promised Ryland she'd find out more information about Rachiah's relationship status, she'd never set foot anywhere near Kyle the next morning.

As it was, her hands shook as she parked her Nissan at Jonesy's barn and climbed out. She didn't want to see Kyle, but she couldn't help looking for him as she walked toward the lower barn doors. The way he'd kissed her, like it was something he couldn't help, had left her more than curious for when he'd do it again and her insides a little unnerved.

He wasn't going to get a chance as far as she was concerned. For the hundred-thousandth time she defended herself with a mental mantra – *I don't string guys along. I don't flirt. It's not my fault. I can't control the way they feel about me.* The things Kyle had said weren't fair. He had to know that.

She checked her watch. Three minutes earlier than they'd agreed. She didn't want to be there any longer than she needed to be. In fact, if Ryland had had a cell phone, she would've just called and shared the information she'd found out. But he didn't and so there she found herself on Saturday, waiting for him to start lunch.

A bench set up outside the double-wide doors offered a place for her to wait. In full view of anyone who rode or walked by.

She sat anyway. He'd promised to meet her there, had begged her to come.

Five minutes became fifteen. Fifteen turned into forty-five.

Why wouldn't she leave? Why hadn't she left yet?

To her shame, she wanted to see Kyle. She just did. She couldn't help it. A part of her wanted to see him so bad. A different part wanted her to cowgirl up and not take that crap from anyone.

Even if he did have the jawline of a young Clint Eastwood and eyes the color of the clearest sky.

She'd just have to work on ignoring the strength in his shoulders and the tenderness in his large hands.

The clip-clopping of horse hooves pulled her attention from the little line of sugar ants working diligently beneath the bench.

Lifting her head, she held her expression neutral as Kyle approached the barn, walking beside a beautiful Arabian horse.

Right behind him, thankfully, was Ryland, covered in sweat and leading a stauncher looking quarter-horse.

Kyle didn't react at seeing her, moving inside the barn like she hadn't sat there at all.

She hid the hurt and smiled largely at Ryland as he approached. She couldn't even be annoyed at his tardiness. She was so distracted on how Kyle messed with her emotions. "You're late."

Ryland glanced past her into the barn. "Yeah, sorry, we've been worked pretty hard this morning since before sun-up." He slouched on the bench beside her and sighed. "Did you find anything out? I need some good news about now."

Sherri grinned. Ryland wasn't interested in her at all and the relaxed friendship they'd developed the other night when he'd stopped by to see Rachiah was a refreshing break from M.T.'s intense expectations.

"I called her this morning and she's not seeing anyone." Sherri grew more serious. "She's pretty focused on this thing with her dad actually. But that doesn't mean she won't be interested when she comes up."

His downtrodden expression brightened. "She's coming back up? When?"

"I'm not sure, but she comes up to visit her mom and step-dad pretty often. We share the place. I can let you know the next time she comes over?" Sherri scratched at the back of her arm.

He leaned forward to stand. Looking down at Sherri, he smiled. "Thanks, Sherri. I mean it. You're a great friend. Rachiah's pretty lucky. Let me know and I'll try to surprise her or something when she gets home." He looked down at his sweat-stained clothes. "I'm going to shower. Thanks again for stopping by. I'll see you later." He nodded at her, his hat dipping and lifting. He led his horse inside and Sherri sighed. All that for less than a minute's worth of conversation.

And less than a handful of seconds of silent rebuke from Kyle.

Standing, Sherri started toward her truck. She was so stupid. Why couldn't she like M.T. the way he liked her? Why couldn't she be like normal women and go for the guy that obviously wanted her? Marry him, have a passel of kids, look forward to growing old together?

Why did she think she had to hold out for the guy who –

"Is that it? That's all you came out here for?" Doubt colored Kyle's tone.

Sherri turned from her walk toward the truck, but she didn't stop. "Don't worry about it. I'd hate to *string* you along." She lifted her chin, then turned back around. Hurt pride fueled the swinging in her arms and her stride.

"Sherri." Regret filled the tone of his one word enough to make her stop.

She crossed her arms, anger more at herself for being weak and not fighting her attraction to him held her muscles tense – even more so than her irritation with him.

She'd never told him about Ryland's interest in Rachiah, but then again, he'd never asked.

His footsteps whispered over the grass as he approached her. "You don't have a thing going on with Ryland? Why didn't you tell me?"

At that Sherri spun, her eyes wide and her lips tight. "Tell you what? We aren't exclusive. Last night was the first time you and I even hung out. You have to admit, coming home and finding a guy in my house with my oven on fire isn't exactly the best start to *any* relationship." Dang him and his masculine scent mixed with the smell of fresh hay. "Plus, let's be honest, it's not like you asked."

A small grin accentuated the smooth bottom curve of his lip as it contrasted with the spiky texture of his skin.

Sherri sighed and crossed her arms over her chest. "Go ahead and laugh." She might reach out and punch him. Just picturing it actually made her feel a little bit better.

"Darlin', you have to admit, there's nothing conventional about us." He pulled her around to face him completely. "At least that guy tried feeding you the most delicious meal full of delicacies you never knew you wanted." His wink brought out a giggle and she covered her mouth.

She couldn't stay mad at him and that irritated her more. "I need to go." Her smile stayed but she turned back to the truck to leave.

"Why? Want to see something?" He reached out and tugged on the upper part of her sleeve.

Did she? What kind of games was he playing now? She didn't resist much as she followed him toward a trail that led off behind the barn toward the mountains.

The lack of rain left the air dry with a breeze that was neither cool nor refreshing, but it stirred the scents of the prairie around them with the heady musky odor of freshly tilled and spread manure.

They walked about twelve-hundred feet in silence. The trail faded into the edge of the woods like a fog in sunlight. Mid-morning light filtered through pine needles and shafted over bark, sending shadows into small crevices.

"It's just over this way." He turned, offering her a small smile as he motioned toward a small collection of trees.

Did she follow him further? She glanced back over the distance they'd come. How taken with him was she?

But his smile promised something special. Sherri didn't have the heart to turn back at that point. She nodded slightly, stepping over the dry needles and grasses on the ground.

"I found this about a week ago, just before meeting you at the bar." He glanced at her quickly then away again.

Curious at his sudden shyness, Sherri ducked between two towering bull pines and pushed past wild huckleberry bushes. The clearing opened up to well-protected velvety soft mullein plants towering above young orange and pink milkweed flowers.

Sherri knelt at the edge of the clearing. She covered her mouth. "Danaus plexippus." The near reverence in her tone leaked from the awe in her heart. Black and orange contrasted sharply together, with small spots of white here and there to add a depth to the wings of the mass of monarch butterflies roosting there in the small safe area.

Kyle crouched beside her, his hands loose between his knees. "What?"

"Monarch butterflies. That's what danaus plexippus is. The larvae and the caterpillars and…" She pointed. "Look, they're resting in the heat." The brightly colored wings flapped but slow, not enough to take flight but enough to stir the air around the beautiful orange and black wings.

The majesty of the clearing captured Sherri's heart. She reached out and held Kyle's hand, basking in the moment of the butterflies. With absolute reverence, she whispered, "They aren't huge up this way, because there isn't a lot of water."

Kyle tapped her arm and pointed with his free hand.

Past the high reaching mullein stalks, the glistening of water trickling into a small pond caught her eye. She didn't want to disturb the butterflies, but she wanted to see that pond. "Is it natural?"

"Yeah, it looks like a collection of underwater streams. The pond isn't deep enough to swim in, but one or two people can probably sit in it with their knees up to their chins." Kyle's chuckle wasn't contained to a whisper and the monarch butterflies rose up from their resting spots in a spectacular cloud of black and orange fluttering lines, and then they settled again.

Sherri watched the wonder on Kyle's face and couldn't hide the wonder on her own. "Thanks for bringing me here. I love this." Not many people understood her fascination with the insect world. Kyle seemed to get it and respect it without a fight. He might not love the tarantula but at least he'd been interested. How many people could say that?

He shrugged, but didn't let go of her hand. "I figured you would." They soaked in the beauty of the moment a little longer until the heat forced them to stand. They stole a few more minutes admiring the view before returning to the trail.

Sherri stopped at the property line. A thick ditch had been dug about five feet wide and a foot deep. She scuffed the toe of her hiking boot in the slightly dried dirt. "You guys listened to me? No one else is taking me seriously." She tried not to show her frustration with the overt sexism the ranch owners had shown. It wasn't their fault they'd never had a female Land Management agent.

Bull crap, sexism shouldn't matter and they were ignoring her warnings because she was a woman.

But Kyle and his cousins hadn't ignored her. The proof was in the freshly dug fire line.

"Of course. We take important information seriously." He squeezed her hand. "Let's go get a drink. I'm sure my break is about up." He tugged her along beside him, grinning as he didn't let go of her hand.

Sherri's heart refused to reject him or the uncertainty of the moment. Every second that passed made Sherri a little bit happier she'd waited to see Ryland.

She would remember that Monarch field for a long, long time.

~~~

Rachiah

There was nothing Rachiah hated more than a guy that pushed her friends for information about her and her dating interests. Of course, that's what was happening with Sherri. Rachiah had no idea who was pushing Sherri for information, but the pointed questions Sherri had called to ask earlier that morning left Rachiah more than a little frustrated.

To the point that she'd called her brother to check in on things.

"M.T., who's hanging around Sherri? Do you know?" Someone was pushing Sherri for information and if anyone knew what was going on with Sherri, it would be Maverick.

"Yeah, those Trails cousins. I'm getting more than a little annoyed with them, Rachiah. They won't leave her alone." M.T.'s growl reverberated across the line.

Rachiah rolled her eyes. "Well, I think they're bugging her about me, to be honest. She called me this morning, asking very pointed questions about my relationship status and if I'm interested in any one in particular. I felt like I was back in middle school."

Relief flooded Maverick's tone. "Oh, they're interested in you? Okay, that makes sense. I can handle that. Then don't worry, 'Chiah. You're not even here for them to bother. I'll take care of it on this end." He laughed and hung up, as if that was the end of the call.

And in a way, maybe it was. Maybe Rachiah would like some help in stifling unwanted attention her way. And maybe, she just wanted to hear her brother's voice. Was there something wrong with wanting to not feel so alone?

Chapter 12

Kyle

Kyle didn't want to wait another six days to see Sherri, but with Nate away with Emma and Sherri's overtime schedule, they didn't have much of a choice.

Friday evening came with a cranky vengeance and Kyle couldn't wait to turn the ranch and its problems over to Jareth. The fire line was still in production along with cougars making a ruckus at the north side of the property.

Leaving the issues in the barn, Kyle splashed some cologne over his neck he borrowed from Damon. Moments later, he revved the engine in ole Betsy in anticipation of seeing Sherri.

He had a fun night planned with her and he couldn't wait to pick her up.

On the main road into the reservation, Kyle avoided making eye contact with M.T. who sat sentinel in a lifted '70's style Bronco with tinted rear windows.

The creepy feeling that he was being watched didn't ebb even as he picked up Sherri in her curve hugging shirt and jeans and wavy hair. Or as they drove off the reservation and there were two more trucks beside M.T., all of them watching like they could see inside Kyle's mind.

Only in the movie theater at Colby did the feeling finally fade enough Kyle could relax.

Sitting beside Kyle in the dark theater, Sherri traced the lines of his wrist with her fingertip and leaned toward him. Whispering wasn't necessary during the previews but Kyle appreciated a reason to lean close enough to smell citronella. Dang, her scent was comforting.

A hand slammed down on his shoulder, squeezing tight on the muscle between his shoulder and neck.

Reflexively, Kyle jumped to his feet, spinning around and jarring the hold from his neck. He scanned the theater to make sure only one man was stupid enough to attempt grabbing him like that and not a group to ambush him. His boots whispered softly over the cement floor of the cinema as he moved.

Guy roostered with his chest out and his chin up. The slope of the theater flooring raised his height to equal that of Kyle's. A little man with a big ego. Guy sneered. "You still hanging with my sloppy seconds?" He cast a sideways glance at Sherri, ogling her before returning his gaze to Kyle. "I didn't realize you were into that. Maybe I need to get your sister again and we can double."

The prodding pushed in just the right spot and Kyle's wound up anger uncoiled. He threw a punch that landed clean below Guy's right eye. The connection reverberated down Kyle's arm and into his chest.

The other man didn't stand a chance and stumbled backwards into the seats behind him.

Members in the waiting audience gasped and a woman screamed as he fell.

Dazed, Guy shook his head, raising his hand to rub at his cheek, staring at the floor for a long moment. As things cleared, he raised his eyes and glared at Kyle. After another moment, he stood, fear holding him back from saying too much, but before he darted from the seating area, he screamed at Kyle with a finger thrusting into the air, "You are so finished, Darby. Done!"

Kyle clenched his fists at his sides, anxious to run after the coward and finish things once and for all, but unwilling to leave Sherri unguarded.

He waited another moment after Guy disappeared and then turned and reclaimed his seat beside Sherri. Kyle offered a tight attempt at a reassuring smile and patted her hand with his. His heart was racing. He had no problem fighting anyone who needed a good whooping, but he didn't want to fight in public. What if a kid saw him and thought it was okay? That didn't sit well with Kyle. His breathing slowed and he sighed.

Sherri didn't let Kyle pull away, but turned her hand over and claimed his fingers in hers. She leaned over and rested her head on the top of his arm. She didn't say anything but Kyle felt like he could see her thoughts and that she was glad he was okay.

He peeked at the top of her head, overcome by an immense desire to tell her he really liked her and loved being around her, but the lights dimmed further, signaling the start of the feature. Maybe he'd tell her after.

They didn't separate their intertwined fingers the length of the film.

~~~

Emma

Emma blinked at the hospital curtains blocking out the little light there was in the rainy Seattle climate. Nate would be there to take her home in less than an hour and she needed to be ready, both physically and mentally.

She was being released after all of her tests had come back negative. How was that possible? Why, if she wasn't sick, did she feel as awful as she had when she was younger, except... worse? Part of her had hoped they were going to tell her she was pregnant when they'd come in and taken her blood for a number of tests. The paperwork had listed pregnancy as one of the tests being done. She'd hoped and prayed that's all that was wrong with her.

Because it wouldn't be *wrong* at all.

Leaning her head back on the soft hospital pillow, Emma focused on the feel of the linen beneath her fingertips and the soft beeping of the monitors beside her bed. They wouldn't remove her IV until she was closer to being released. She was counting down the hours. Soon, it would be minutes and then she could go back home with her husband.

Since Nate had been with her at the hospital all that time, Emma had only been able to be herself and succumb to her pain and fatigue when he was asleep, in the cafeteria, or even visiting the restroom. She'd asked him to grab her things from her parents' place first thing that morning before she and Nate went home to Montana.

Emma needed a chance to get her head on straight. She breathed in deep, closing her eyes. She was getting released. She could go home. That's all she needed to do – be at home. The doctors didn't know what was wrong with her which meant Emma just needed a chance to rest. That's it. Maybe she could work on getting more vitamins or something. Maybe more sunlight. She had no idea what was making her so weak or nauseous, or even causing the splitting migraines, but the doctors said nothing was wrong. So, maybe nothing was wrong.

Except, deep down inside, Emma knew that wasn't true.

Opening her eyes at the sound of movement coming from the doorway, Emma bit back a grimace. She wasn't ready for Nate to be back yet. She really did need a little bit of time without him hovering. She could only pretend to be doing just fine for so long.

Instead of the arrival being Nate, Dr. Derry stood in her doorway, hesitancy in the way he stood half-in and half-out across the threshold. He gave Emma a smile that promised nothing good was in his daily report.

Holding a clipboard in his hands as he approached, Dr. Derry cleared his throat and came to a stop beside her bed. "Good morning, Emma. How are you today?" The question was extra fluff that neither of them cared enough about to answer or even wait for a reply.

Emma blinked, shaking her head. "I was *fine*, but judging by the expression on your face, I'm about to barely hold onto *okay*." She grinned, but her lips trembled. "Go ahead, Dr. Derry. Don't hold back. I've been through this enough times, I know you have news."

The doctor shifted uncomfortably and sighed. He glanced around the hospital room and furrowed his brow. Tapping the clipboard on his open palm, he pressed his lips together. "Do we need to wait for Nate?" Was that hope in the doctor's tone?

Shaking her head tightly, Emma weakly tried to shift herself up higher in the bed. "No. I'd rather not. Can you just let me know so I can... process it?" Whatever *it* was. She took a deep breath and held it, counting in her head how long it took for Dr. Derry to come clean with the problem.

One.

Two.

Three. Four. Five.

Seven.

He finally gripped the clipboard in both hands and tucked his chin. "Well, I'm just going to cut to the chase." He blinked and nodded. "The tests from last week were a false negative. The cancer is back and it's going to be harder to treat this time since it's in Stage III." He lamely claimed pamphlets from his clipboard and tried offering them to her.

But Emma just stared blankly at the doctor. After a minute, she nodded, her breathing shallow and short. "I knew... I knew something was wrong. I just... didn't think it was really going to be that." She blinked and folded her arms across her chest. She lifted her chin. "Okay, so what are my treatment options? What do I need to do?"

But honestly? She didn't want to. If the cancer was worse, then that meant her quality of life was going to be worse, not to mention the treatment would be more intense, more expensive and take even more from her husband than she already had.

She couldn't do that to Nate. He already worked so hard. They were just barely staying afloat. The medical bills alone would eat the whole last years' worth of increase.

Her stomach sank. She swallowed, her mouth dry from the medications they'd been giving her to control her nausea. She wanted to tell the doctor she didn't want to know the options. She didn't want to know anything except what time Nate was coming for her.

And maybe, how much longer they had together.

That last thought lodged a lump in her throat and she worked her mouth to say something. Blinking back tears, she forced a smile, waiting for Dr. Derry's answer.

But just how much did she really want to know? Whatever he was going to tell her, she wanted him to hurry and get out. She didn't want Nate to know about the updates. If she could keep things a secret, maybe she could stave off the inevitable.

Because it was inevitable. She could feel it. A good outcome wasn't going to be likely. Not this time around. Not when she was barely holding on as it was.

Home. She just wanted to get home. Everything was better at Bella Acres.

Chapter 13

Sherri

Monday dawned sooner than Sherri was ready for. She couldn't call Kyle first thing, like she wanted to since he was already out on the ranch. Dang, she wouldn't even see him until the next Friday again.

She'd moved back to Clearwater County to be around family and have more time to do the things she wanted to, spend time with those she wanted to, but with the Western Pine Beetle infestation she was working overtime. Her findings made the ranchers work longer – which meant Kyle worked longer.

She removed her wide work hat and closed the office door behind her. Cool air conditioning soothed the morning heat from her flushed face.

Barry Fielding rushed in, his bald crown freckled and white shining under the fluorescent lights. "This week is raring to be a scorcher. I'm closing the parks. There are already some real burners over in northern Idaho and Wyoming is getting hit as well." His hands trembled as he talked about the only real excitement he ever saw in his job.

"Did you want me to go close the entrances?" Closing the parks fell under her responsibilities. She wouldn't mind hitting the ridge anyway, a chance to catch a glimpse of Kyle more motivation at the moment. Plus, if she could close the parks and lessen the chance at fire mishaps, she'd do what she needed to.

"You don't mind? Why don't you close the northern parks and I'll close the southern ones? The state already closed the ones running along I-90 further south." He poured a cup of coffee from the complimentary carafe set up on a small buffet in the corner. The Styrofoam cup fit his hand and he used a red stirrer to mix in powdered creamer from a single use packet. He sipped the steaming drink and screwed his lips up to the side. "Ew, that's bitter."

Sherri laughed. The coffee had been sitting there since Friday. He'd commented on the taste versus the fact that it was probably ice cold. She moved away from the window and narrowed her eyes at her boss. "When did you want to start?"

Grinning, Barry looked up from his cup. "You're still here?"

Taking the hint, Sherri grabbed the keys to the truck issued to her. "I'll radio when I'm headed back to the office."

He nodded as he poured the dregs of his cup into the water fountain beside the door. Maybe the temperature was more of a problem then he was letting on. Or maybe he'd make a new pot.

The drive out to the park was uneventful, much to Sherri's disappointment. She tried, but no sign of Kyle on the sunlit prairies left her discouraged and more than a little deflated.

At the turnout, she parked the truck and grabbed a fanny pack with water and jerky and headed up the trail.

About two miles in, a rest stop provided respite from the heat. But the doors on the small building needed to be checked as well as the remainder of the trails. Since she was up there, she might as well gather any samples that she needed, too.

She'd only been up that far looking for the hikers the week before. She wanted to get some samples of the Western Pine Beetles to gauge growing patterns.

They seemed rather aggressive for the time of year and the area.

Not too long ago, she'd read about the influx of varying organisms due to increases and decreases in water and temperatures, but she'd never seen the beetles affected so distinctly and in such a concentrated amount.

Up ahead of her on the trail, within view of the bright blue port-a-potty, a man and a woman waved their arms frantically. From the distance, voices called but the words were swept away by the wind and absorbed by pine needles.

Sherri picked up her pace, slowing when she reached them. "Are you alright? What's going on?"

The man wiped tears from his eyes. "Our horse…" His sobs caught up his words and he choked. He gripped the woman's hand in his, his knuckles whitening with the pressure. "I won't do it, Margaret. If we have to put him down… I can't do it."

His companion placed a hand on his upper arm and with tears in her eyes, pointing down the side of the hill toward untraveled terrain. "The gelding is down there."

Sherri's eyes widened and she nodded, more to reassure herself than them. Ever since Cyan's dog passed away a year or so ago, Sherri was afraid of seeing animals dead or injured. She could handle the death of most things creepy, crawly, and with more than four legs, but things that made noises? Not so much.

Thick leaves on wild currant bushes blocked her view and she pushed at them as she carefully stepped off the shoulder of the path. She glanced back at the couple standing with their arms around each other. If she was like Rachiah and took horror movies to heart, she wouldn't even think about going into those woods alone. But this was Sherri and she laughed at Stephen King's *It* because if spiders didn't scare her – what would?

Besides fire. Stephen King's *Carrie* had scared the bejunkers out of her. Rachiah didn't need to know that, though. Sherri would never hear the end of it, if Rachiah knew.

Sherri held onto a protruding root from a nearby pine as she scrabbled down the steep slope into the mini-valley.

The complete lack of sound chilled her blood. No thrashing, no screams, nothing.

Had they made it up? Were they lying? Why would they do that? They both seemed genuinely upset.

Sherri stepped further down the hill, disbelief slowly growing in her gut. At the crux of the valley, she stood with her hands on her hips and surveyed as much as she could see, but nothing seemed out of the ordinary.

She sighed, long and low and turned to go when a brown chestnut rear-end caught her eye from the protection of brush and grasses. Had the horse died?

Moving closer, she was careful not to make any loud sounds or sudden movements. Searching the animal with her gaze, she pushed the leaves away, checking for signs of life. Dirt covered his coat like he'd flipped down the side of the hill. Looking back up the way she'd come, Sherri grimaced.

Coming down, she hadn't noticed the bent branches and smashed bushes. She'd been too concerned with getting down the steep embankment herself.

At the head of the horse, she searched his open eyes which flickered as she moved in his line of vision. But he didn't move. Didn't whimper.

Nothing.

She wasn't a veterinarian. She didn't know what to do. Pulling out her phone, she tried calling Barry but only got his voicemail – all three times she called him.

Finally, she dialed Cyan.

"Cyan, I need help. I'm on Beaver Ridge and there's a downed horse up this way. Not moving, but his eyes are open. I think he's in pain." She contained her own whimpers as she waited for Cyan to tell her what to do.

"Holy cow, Sherri. Okay, I'll call you back in a second." Cyan hung up, not even waiting for a goodbye.

Sherri crouched down beside the large animal. She didn't want to touch him in case it hurt him more, but she didn't want to leave him either. No one should be alone in that much pain. "Sh. It's okay."

Sh? *Sh* to who? He was barely breathing with how still he was.

Her phone dinged in her hand. She hurriedly answered and pressed the cell to her ear. "Yeah?"

"I called Kyle. He's the closest. Jareth is at Jonesy's, but the closest vet is a doc in Colby, um, a McAllister or something. He'll talk to Kyle by phone and walk him through what to do." Cyan's businesslike tone was normal when she panicked for her friends. The woman had an ability to keep her calm in the most extraordinary of circumstances.

Sherri nodded numbly. "Okay. Is Kyle heading up the hill? I can shoot off an emergency flare. No, wait." She shook her head. "I can't do that. Fire danger."

"I'm sure he'll find you. I told him off the trail. He's pretty capable. I'll keep my line clear. Call me as soon as you're able." She hung up, leaving Sherri grateful she didn't have to worry about small talk as she sat next to a horribly injured animal.

Where had the owners gone? They hadn't followed her down and she didn't want to leave the big animal to retrieve them.

The minutes passed like hours and days. She didn't check the time but instead stared at the horse and his eyes as he tried to focus on something or anything, his safety instincts on high alert. His ears flicked forward and back. And still, no sound.

After what could have been two lifetimes, Kyle appeared in the V of the valley on his horse who carefully picked its way over the natural debris on the forest floor.

Kyle was there. Even though Cyan had *said* he would come, the bleakness of the situation hadn't seemed to allow room for the brightness the thought of Kyle would bring. And yet there he was.

Sherri stood slowly, wiping her moist palms on the tops of her jeans, relieved to see him.

He slid from the Arabian and handed Sherri the rope. Slowly, he approached the gelding and knelt beside him. Keeping his voice low, Kyle murmured, "Can I borrow your phone? I'm supposed to call the vet."

Sherri held out her hand, a little disappointed he hadn't greeted her differently and yet fully aware that she didn't know how to greet him either. An urgent situation called for a more controlled emotional response.

But that didn't mean Sherri didn't want to be grabbed and kissed. It just meant that she understood why she hadn't.

He dialed a number by memory and spoke with someone on the other line. Sherri could only assume it was the veterinarian.

Kyle stated things he saw and then ran his hands carefully down legs and sides. The belly of the horse moved as he breathed, sometimes quickly and shallowly and sometimes slow and deep.

Kyle nodded after he reported his findings. He fell quiet and just listened, softly stroking the horse's mane and watching his eyes.

After a moment of listening he finished with, "Yes, I understand. Thank you." He handed the phone to Sherri who pushed the end button.

"Doctor McAllister said he most likely broke his pelvis. He also said that we need to stay with him until he can get a helicopter up here to airlift the poor guy out." Kyle stroked the horse's jowls. "It's okay, buddy." He looked up at Sherri. "Where are the owners?"

She pointed weakly up where she'd left them. "They were up that way, but I'm not sure if they still are."

"Let's hope they didn't abandon him. If not, I'll call my friends at the horse rescue ranch and see what they can do to help." He clenched his jaw, a small tic in movement just at the curve pulling her gaze like a magnet.

Sherri sat Indian-style on the soft ground. "Thank you for coming. I know you're busy at the ranch. I called Cyan because I didn't know what to do—" She was rambling and she knew it. Her adrenaline had taken over and her hands shook.

Kyle shifted his weight to put him closer to Sherri. He rested his finger against her lips. "It's okay. I think you did the best you could and I'm glad I could help." He winked, his smile sad but in place.

"But you have to admit, you were just trying to see me before Friday."

Even under the circumstances, Sherri couldn't contain a grin. "What makes you think you're seeing me Friday?" His confidence relieved her. At least one of them was confident.

"What makes you think I'm not?" He leaned closer to her and pushed his lips against hers, just enough to brush warm skin across the sensitive flesh of her lower lip. He pulled back and winked at her. In mock horror, he continued speaking low. "How dare you try to take advantage of me and my emotions for this poor creature?"

"You're sweet to try to distract me." She sobered and studied the horse. "Did the vet say how long?"

"No, he has to make some calls first. I can make some calls, too, and get my jobs covered. Do you need to call your boss?" He tilted his head. "I assume we're staying together?" The warm invitation was in his eyes and Sherri couldn't say no, even if she wanted to.

They made their calls and other than concern for the horse, no one gave them any problems or expected any less than staying with an injured animal – whether they owned the creature or not.

Together, Sherri and Kyle claimed a spot on crushed down ferns and tall grasses beside the heavy breathing horse.

"I wish we could do something to help him. He has to be in so much pain." Sherri rested her chin on her knees pulled up to her chest. "He's got to be so scared."

"I can't believe those people never came back for him. He's a beautiful horse. What do you think his name is?" Kyle petted the large animal's nose with care, speaking low and comforting.

Sherri picked at a stalk of grass, flicking the pieces into the surrounding foliage. She considered the horse and its richly brown coat. "He's a big strong guy and if he survives this, he should be named something like Duke or Maxximus." She shrugged. "I'm not the best at naming things."

"I think those are great names." Kyle studied the big brown eyes and whispered, "I think Duke is a perfect name."

"Duke it is." Sherri's heart tingled at the sight of Kyle leaning over the fallen horse with the Arabian nibbling on green grass just past the dark brim of his Stetson.

She'd be very irritated if she fell for Kyle and ended up crushed worse than the horse.

Unbridled Trails

Chapter 14

Kyle

Spending more than a handful of hours with Sherri in the woods and nothing else to do but watch an injured horse was exactly what Kyle needed. Not necessarily the injured horse part, but anything with Sherri was enjoyable, even that.

The delicate way she touched her forehead with the back of her thumb to sweep her hair away entranced him. She had an ability to captivate others –

him especially. He wasn't surprised M.T. was so taken with her.

Kyle pulled his knees up and wrapped his arms around them, rocking back slightly to watch her as they talked. "This whole M.T. thing. Is he going to back off?" How long would Kyle have to watch his back with the tribal man?

Sherri's laugh brightened the woods around them. "Doubtful. He's professed his 'undying love' for years. He doesn't have anyone to compare me to. Once he gets out there and sees more of the world, he'll understand there's nothing special about me." A derisive smile and a wave of her fingers enunciated her comment. "I mean, I'm just an entomologist. My idea of a good time is sitting around feeding crickets to Tommy. Or going for a hike. Maverick has different ideas and he's idolized me. It's not as serious as he thinks it is."

"Isn't Tommy the spider that tried to kill me?" Kyle made his eyes grow wide in mock terror. He'd never live down the way he reacted to the monster. Might as well play it up.

"Hardly." She giggled and Kyle couldn't help it. He pulled her closer, to sit beside him. She fit against his side like she was made to be there. And maybe she had. Maybe everything about her was supposed to complement Kyle.

The sound of helicopter blades beating the air grew, interrupting the moment.

Kyle met Sherri's dark eyes and murmured, "You're growing on me, bug girl."

For a moment, he thought she might reply in kind, until she pulled back, her eyes downcast as she scooted a couple inches from him. "You don't want that. I'm serious when I say, I'm boring." She directed her gaze upward, trying to see through the towering canopy of pine boughs. She cleared her throat and pointed at the sky. "Which way will they come from?"

Bemused, Kyle considered her, not looking up when he pointed southwest. She continued avoiding his eyes. Why did she pull away when he mentioned anything remotely intimate? She didn't strike him as a girl who had relationship problems. Kyle wasn't one to hide from talking things out. Much to his brother's irritation.

"Sherri, I don't want to push, but why do you pull away when I try to get closer?" Kyle reached out again, touching her hand softly with the tips of his fingers.

She glanced down, but made an obvious effort to not pull away. Sherri still didn't meet his gaze. "It's really not you. It's just… guys don't like me. They like what they think they can do to me. I'm not the exotically angry one of my group of friends like Rachiah. I'm not the eccentrically principled one like Cyan. I'm just…" She shrugged, her cheeks pink. "Mild. I'm a vegan who doesn't like it spicy. Bugs have always been a passion of mine. Boys? Not so much. I just don't see the point in being tied down to someone who doesn't like the same things as me." She smiled softly, wrinkling her nose. "I don't mean to be blunt, but you can't even talk about Tommy without goosebumps."

Kyle cleared his throat, inclining his head. "You have to admit, he's huge."

Sherri burst out laughing. "Yes, he definitely has size on his side."

"So, you're saying the only thing you like are bugs." Kyle didn't want to miss a flicker of an eyelash or a curl of her lips. She was opening up to him and he didn't want to lose the opportunity to figure out how he could get closer without pushing her away.

She blinked like she was taken by surprise. "No. Actually I like a lot of things."

It was Kyle's turn to laugh. "Let's build on the things we have in common rather than run from the things we don't then. Name a couple of things you like and I'll let you know if I agree or disagree." He'd lie, if he had to.

She considered him, ignoring the chopping of blades above their small clearing. Slowly she nodded. "Okay. I can do that. I like horses." She cast a sympathetic glance at the gelding resting beside them.

Kyle reached out and flipped a stray chunk of hair off her cheek. "Good. So do I." At least they had that in common. He liked a good steak while she preferred tofu. "Do you like chocolate?"

Sherri rolled her eyes and jutted her jaw to the side. "Everyone likes chocolate."

Keeping his facial expression stoic, Kyle shook his head. "Not true. I don't like it."

Shock smoothed the humor from Sherri's features. She blinked repeatedly at him as she took in what he'd said. "You really don't? I mean, I didn't think that was possible." She sank back, disappointment strong in the slouch of her shoulders and the way she tucked her chin.

It was Kyle's turn to laugh. He leaned over, bumping her shoulder with his and snickering. "Of course, I like chocolate. But wow, now I know just how important the treat is to you. You were ready to get up and abandon me here." He chuckled when she playfully reached out and punched him in the upper arm.

"Not really. I was just trying to picture my life without chocolate. I have to be honest, I'm not sure I could do it." Sherri grinned sheepishly as she returned to her original position.

"Well, if we're going to get right down to it, you've chosen to live without bacon. If you can do that, you can do anything." Kyle watched the delight in her eyes as they talked about the things they both liked.

As far as he was concerned, they had more in common than they were going to admit. Or she was going to admit.

He just had to figure out a way to convince her he wasn't like other guys. Because she was definitely not like other women.

~~~

Kyle didn't get back to the bunkhouse for dinner until the guys were heading up for seconds and dessert. His thirst was undeniable so he headed straight for the water at an empty seat by Nate. He glanced at his older cousin in surprise and delight. "Hey, when did you get back?" Things had to be going well, if Nate was home already.

Nate's eyes were shadowed and ringed as he looked up from the food he swirled around his plate with his fork. He spoke with a voice that was husky and worn like he'd gargled with whiskey and glass. "Yeah, well, the cancer's back. And Emma just wanted to be home, so…" He trailed off, forcing a bite into his mouth and sipping a drink he obviously didn't want.

Kyle sank onto the seat beside him, his euphoria over Sherri shrinking into a black pit of despair. "It's back?" More cousins closed rank as they heard Kyle's voice. Murmurs of sadness and regret surrounded them.

Nate nodded, baring his teeth but unable to pull off even a fake smile. "Yeah, but we'll beat it, right? That's what she and I do. We beat it." He hung his head and then lifted his chin, tears bright in his eyes. "Except... this time... she didn't even tell me. She wants to keep it a secret. The doctor pulled me aside and said he'd told her and..." He curled in on himself, his arms folded as if he could protect himself from the pain.

"Why are you here? I mean, why aren't you with Emma?" Kyle didn't touch his water. He couldn't care about his thirst when his cousin hurt so much. All of them hurt at the news of one of their own getting such debilitating news.

Nate sniffed, shaking his head. "She… well, she thinks I'm convinced nothing is wrong and that I don't know anything. So, she sent me back here and refuses to admit that anything is wrong. If she doesn't want to talk about it or do anything about it, I can't force it. Plus…" Nate cleared his throat, trying to straighten his back and his shoulders. "Maybe… maybe if we ignore it, then it won't be real, right? I mean… she's been through this before. If she ignores it, then maybe it will go away. There has to be a reason she just wants to leave it for now."

A solid mass settled in Kyle's stomach. What would happen to the cousins if Emma didn't pull out of this one? What emptiness would they all face? Just the thought of losing Emma was more than he could imagine. He blinked as he struggled to get away from the thoughts of losing her.

"Can we talk about something else?" Nate motioned toward the rest of the ranch hands who had grown quiet while he spoke. He obviously wanted to get the attention off him.

Searching for a topic to switch to, Kyle swallowed. "We just saved a horse. Do you guys know what happens to a horse if it's injured and no one claims it?" He looked around at the group. Someone had to know something.

Andy, a new ranch hand recently hired, spoke up. "They usually euthanize it. If the owner abandons it and there's no one to pay the bills, well, you know. They don't waste the funds when they can get more money from turning it into feed." He shrugged and stuffed a gravy dipped biscuit in his mouth.

Euthanized? Kyle had never had his own horse, but he couldn't see letting a beautiful horse like Duke die because of owners who didn't want it or didn't want the bills associated with fixing it.

Could he just toss an animal aside like that? Emotionally he had more invested in that horse than any other animal before. Maybe because he'd bonded more with Sherri over the injured animal and its circumstances or maybe because he'd had to drop everything and be there for something besides himself or the Montana Trails or his family or his sister. He was doing it for altruistic purposes… or was he?

He would have something in common with Sherri. They liked horses. But at the same time, he was sick of not having anything of his own. Taking a horse from job to job wasn't as difficult as it might seem. A lot of ranches liked when you brought your own ride with you. Kyle might have to look into the injured horse. One way or the other, he had to figure out a way to help the animal. He couldn't let it get turned into dog food. He just couldn't.

What about a person? Emma was sick and she was ignoring the problem. Nate was letting her. What would Kyle do in that situation? Could he ignore the situation and wait to see if it would get better?

Wasn't that what he was doing with Ruby?

Emma's health problems reminded Kyle how fragile they all were. He excused himself and made his way to the phone by the front door. The situation with his cousin-in-law reminded him of the problems with his sister that he'd been ignoring. He might not want to reach out, but he had to admit – at least in the depths of his heart – that if he didn't make a move, nothing might ever happen.

He'd regret his decision not to do anything for the rest of his life. He dialed his sister's number by heart, even though they hadn't spoken in quite a while.

She picked up on the first ring. "Kyle?" The delighted surprise in her voice brought a smile to Kyle's lips. He'd missed her and he hated that he'd waited as long as he had to check in on her.

He cleared his throat, hoping his emotions weren't betrayed by his voice. "Hey, Rubics. How you doin'?"

She half-laughed and half-cried. "I can't believe you finally called me back." She sniffed, not trying even half as hard as Kyle was to contain her emotions.

Narrowing his eyes, Kyle ducked his head to hear better. "Called you back? What are you talking about?" He turned to lean against the wall, watching his cousins and the other ranch hands from his vantage point.

"I asked Mom to have you call me. I don't even know how many times." Her whisper carried over the line and she sniffed again.

"She never told me. Why weren't you at the wedding?" He didn't mention all the Thanksgivings and Christmases she'd missed over the years. He knew why she hadn't been there. Their parents weren't the most loving people or the most understanding.

"You know why. Mom can't even look at me and Dad's pretty much disowned me." Her weak laugh made him twist his lips.

He sighed at the truth in her words. "But it wasn't your fault." Kyle hung his head, his chin almost to his chest. "They didn't invite you? Mom said you got an invitation and that it was your choice not to go."

"No, I got an invitation the same day I got a note from Mom telling me not to come. She didn't want to cast a shadow on Jareth's big day." She laughed, whether at herself or the situation or something else, the sound lacked humor. "Because I'm an embarrassment."

"You don't embarrass me." He rubbed his elbow. His poor sister. She didn't deserve to be a victim and also be shamed. Jareth hadn't said anything to Kyle about the situation. Hopefully, he didn't know. Either that or he accepted the lies their mother told, too. Was that so far-fetched? Hadn't Kyle initially believed everything their mother had said, too?

"Thanks, Kyle. So, what's with the call? You have to have a reason for reaching out." She brightened her tone.

"I just wanted to share some fun news with you. I met someone. She's different and she likes bugs." His grin erupted at just the thought of Sherri and talking about her with his sister solidified the idea that welled in his chest. He could be falling for her and he didn't know if he wanted that or not.

"That's great, Kyle. I'm so happy. I'm expecting a letter with detailed descriptions of her and things you guys have done together." Her giggle lightened as she talked about a car show she was planning on attending that upcoming weekend and more crazy stuff going on at their relatives' home.

Kyle talked some more with his sister, feeling for the briefest moment like she wasn't as far away as she really was. One way or the other, he had to get her and bring her back to be with Jareth and him. They needed their sister.

As he turned while talking, Kyle caught a glimpse of Nate's downtrodden expression. Was falling for someone something to be happy about? Or was Kyle destined to be weighted down with heartache like Nate? Kyle didn't know if he'd ever feel for someone like Nate did and he didn't want to face losing anyone.

What if that's what happened when you fell for someone? Maybe you lost faith in the person you chose because they let you down, like his own parents. Or maybe one got sick, or they got hurt, or they became unhappy and they left.

Kyle didn't want to lose Sherri. For any reason.

Chapter 15

Sherri

"I'm fine. Do you want me to come to the office, Barry?" Sherri stopped at the intersection where one direction led home and the other way led to work. She rubbed at her forehead, very tired at the day's events so far.

"No, I'm glad you're fine and that horse is getting care. Great job today. We'll see you in the morning." He hung up, probably eating dinner. At least she could be glad he was a man of few words.

Sherri sighed, relieved to be headed home. But she hadn't closed the trail. She hadn't finished her job. She'd have to turn back and finish that up before she went home.

Her cell rang. She glanced at the caller ID before answering. "Cyan, how's it going?" Sherri turned the rig around and glanced in the mirror to check for oncoming traffic, not that she expected much around that time of day clear out where she was.

"Are you still out? Stop by and eat with me. Jareth isn't home yet." Cyan's soft demand hid something.

Sherri was tired but not so tired she couldn't be there for her friend. "I'll be there in a little bit. You still at Emma's?" She'd have time to close the trail afterward. She turned again, more than ready to do what was needed.

"Yeah, see you in a little bit." Cyan never said goodbye and Sherri appreciated it. The drive there wouldn't take long, but would be enough for Sherri to dwell on her time with Kyle.

The man was enough to keep her on her toes, keep her interested, but was *she* enough to keep him interested?

He liked her, but she didn't want him to get bored. What if she got so attached to him that when he stopped liking her, her heart broke? Wasn't she falling for him already?

No, she couldn't be. She didn't want to be that dependent on anyone.

She pulled into Nate's place and parked. A sense of foreboding stayed her hand as she waited a moment before opening the door. Why had Cyan's voice sounded tight and why didn't she ask about the horse or Kyle?

Sherri knocked on the front door. She picked at the inner soft skin of her thumb. Something wasn't right and Sherri was worried Cyan only involved her because it was so very bad.

Cyan pulled open the door, a sad smile on her lips. She spoke softly and leaned on the panel as she held it open. "Hey, thanks for coming over."

"What's going on?" Sherri's eyes widened as Cyan pulled her to the side of the front door just outside.

She snapped the door shut softly and glanced around behind her like someone might be lurking. Turning back to Sherri, Cyan kept her voice low even while the intensity matched the demand in her gaze. "I need you to tell Emma what's been going on with you and Kyle. She needs something to take her mind off…" Cyan blinked away tears. She continued in a whisper. "The cancer's back. Nate… I don't know if he knows, but Hannah called and told me. She found the paperwork when she was helping unload Emma's things from her stay in the hospital." Cyan exhaled on a whoosh and pressed at the skin beneath her eyes.

Nodding, Sherri bit her lip. "Oh, I'm so sorry. Okay, of course, I can talk about it." She followed

Cyan inside. What was going on between her and Kyle and how did everyone know?

Cyan led Sherri further into the house, stopping inside the front living room. Emma sat on a couch with her arms wrapped around a throw pillow, staring blankly out the window.

"Hi Emma, how's it going?" Sherri smiled, unsure what to say or what to do. She didn't know Emma well, but she'd always liked the woman who seemed to lead the cousins at Nate's side. They all loved Emma, evident in the way they talked about her went out of their way to take care of her when they were around.

Laughing, Cyan shook her head and rolled her eyes. "Emma, Sherri was just telling me about Kyle coming to help rescue a horse up on Beaver Ridge." Cyan rubbed her lips together and widened her eyes at Sherri as she moved further into the room.

Turning from the window, Emma glanced toward Sherri. She spoke slowly, dark shadows under her eyes. "Kyle, huh? Tell me more about what you and Kyle were up to." She didn't seem morose and instead exuded sincere interest in what Sherri had to say.

An hour passed of Sherri telling her story and Emma asking pointed questions about Kyle and, more importantly, Sherri's interaction with him. They were laughing like school girls when Jareth walked in.

He pulled the hat from his head, pausing and looking back out the door and then back at them. "Am I in the right place?" He furrowed his brow, but Sherri couldn't tell if it was in jest or from serious confusion.

Cyan stood to kiss Jareth on the lips. "Hey, where'd you go? I thought you were going to come right home after dinner at the ranch? Hannah made dinner and we have more than we need. You're supposed to come help us eat it so her feelings don't get hurt."

"I heard that!" Hannah called from the kitchen, her words bringing a smile to everyone's face.

Jareth peeked at Emma and then glanced back at Cyan. "Yeah, well, Nate wanted to have a meeting about the upcoming branding of the young cattle and I couldn't say no. We haven't seen him in a while." He cleared his throat and glanced more decisively at Emma. "How are you feeling, Em? You've been gone a while."

No mention of Kyle and what he and Sherri had been up to. Had Kyle just not mentioned it to Jareth or was Jareth being discreet? Or maybe Sherri was imagining the import of everything she thought had happened.

Nate stomped through the door, his bandana dark in spots from sweat. "I got the animals fed really fast. Is Sherri still here?" He yanked his hat off as he came inside, hooking the bucket on a hook protruding from the wall beside the doorway.

He spied her and moved closer, ignoring the dirt flecking from his boots to the hardwood floor. He came within inches of her, peering into Sherri's face, his eyes bloodshot in his pale face. "Sherri, do you know anything about leaching?"

"Nathan. That's enough." Emma half-stood from the couch, looking stronger than anyone in that room. "I told you to stop this time. Nothing is wrong. I'm fine. I'm just tired."

"You're not fine. I talked to Dr. Derry at the hospital, Emma. I know. I *know.* You *can't* hide this from me. I'm your husband." Nate thrust his jaw to the side, his arms wide.

"Stop. Fine, you know. Big deal. I'm not hiding anything except... I'm more hoping that you don't know. That's all. It's not like the disease is anything new. It's just a lot worse. Okay? That's it. Nothing else has changed." Emma lifted her chin and stared down her nose at Nate, as if challenging him. "I'm fine."

"We can beat this. Dr. Derry said it's a four-month procedure. We can stay at your parents' place. I heard that leaching might work. I've heard of a lot of things we can try. Maybe Sherri can help us… I mean, we can't give up. We can't quit." Nate blinked back tears, his eyes bright with his frustration and desperation. "No. Not this time. You're not fine. I'm not stopping. Not ever. I'm not quitting. I'm not giving up."

She dropped her hands to her side and crossed the room, lifting her hand to his cheek when she stepped close to his frame. "Aw, Nate. I love you, but this isn't your decision." Her eyes welled with tears. "This is… my decision. I know what will work and what won't. I can feel it. I won't survive anymore treatment. My body… is tired." She screwed her lips to the side and shook her head, glancing at the floor. After a painful moment, she tossed an awkward apology into the room before disappearing up the stairs with her hand pressed to her mouth.

After she left, the room took on a vacuum feel. Nate's shoulders slumped and he pinched his brow. "Sorry, but…" He sighed. "I… I'm sorry to put you in that position, Sherri. I… I'd heard about it from another one of the hands and…" He caught his breath.

Sherri placed her hand on his upper arm and slightly turned him to face her. "It's okay. I understand wondering about leaching." Her tone became that of a teacher's. "Leaching isn't used for cancer, Nate. It's more for relieving fevers or infectious areas. Even if she had those symptoms, I would think she would want every bit of her blood because of the white blood cells."

She glanced between Cyan and Jareth. "I don't know any more than that because I didn't go further with my anatomy and physiology than the basic classes. At least for humans." Her lame laugh fell into the disappointed living room amongst the couches and armchairs. "I'm sorry."

Nate nodded the slightest amount. "So, it's just an old wives' tale. They said that… the doctors, but I just…" He lifted his hand and then let it fall limply to his side.

"She's going to be okay. She's beat it before. She can beat it again." Cyan linked her arm with Sherri's as if they were the solitary force Emma would need to beat her sickness.

"Yeah. She has. But she *wanted* to fight then." He softly shook his head, reaching up to run his fingers through his hair. "She doesn't want to fight anymore." His red-rimmed eyes seemed to beg for help while the slouch in his spine suggested he'd given up, too. "I'm desperate for… something. Maybe an answer I can get without hurting her with modern medicine? If you guys hear anything about natural or alternative treatments, let me know, okay?"

He didn't wait for their acceptance, just turned and walked back outside.

Cyan stared after him while Sherri shifted on her feet.

Sherri liked Emma. If Sherri didn't get things under control with Kyle, she'd be entering a family who could be losing a very important member soon. Sherri didn't want to get that invested. She didn't want to lose anyone. Not when she had never lost anyone her entire life.

She didn't need anyone and she wanted to keep it that way.

But she had a sinking suspicion her heart was already claimed by Kyle and his charismatic family. She'd have to work on that. Vulnerability with people wasn't her thing.

~~~

"I'm going to check on the trails. I didn't get a chance to close them all the way yesterday." Sherri tapped the edge of the phone and watched the road. Barry had called to figure out her plans for the day since he'd been late getting into the office that morning.

"Well, it's no wonder. You had a busy day yesterday. Check and see if there's any further beetle damage, too. I've been fielding calls from ranchers all week, asking me if it's true. Beetles scare them, but apparently a woman warning them is even scarier." He sighed, and Sherri could picture him standing by the window with a hand on his hip. "Keep me updated."

Subtle feminism bothered Sherri but at least it didn't keep Barry from hiring a woman.

"Sure, thanks, Barry." She hung up, placing her phone on the passenger seat. She hadn't slept well with worried thoughts about how she felt for Kyle and what kind of worry Cyan and everyone else seemed to have for Emma. Emma herself seemed more normal than the rest of them.

A car pulled in behind her on the road from the intersection she passed. Tight on her bumper, the car stuck with her. She waved them around, but they didn't move. She was most likely dealing with an angry rancher who didn't want her making demands on his ranch for fire safety. How many times had she dealt with that anger?

They would get bored and then move on. The roads were wide enough to pass. She'd slow down and let them go by in a moment. Either way, she wasn't going to worry about a car when she was in a bigger rig and had a lot on her mind.

She took the next left, turning up the road, passing Jonesy's Acres and keeping an eye out for Kyle. She wouldn't mind seeing him again, especially so soon after their time together the day before.

He liked her, even though they had a lot of differences. The fact that he was willing to work on things they had in common mattered more than she could tell him.

As she got a little further from the intersection, she pulled to the side to let the car pass, but the vehicle slowed and didn't move on. Sherri clutched the wheel and pulled out again. The road was going to get narrower. She'd never be able to turn around to go back without getting stuck in a ditch.

Maybe the other car was going further than the trailheads. She couldn't get out of the truck, if the other car stopped when she did. After that incident with Kyle at the cinemas, she didn't trust that people weren't completely off their saddles.

Angry ranchers could be volatile. She should have pulled into Jonesy's Acres and let the car do what it needed to.

Trees bordering the road pulled back from the shoulder as the turnout to the gravel parking lot came into view.

Turning the wheel, Sherri muttered to know one in particular, "Keep driving. Creep…" But her words trailed off when the car stopped and then sped down the road.

"Okay, whatever. So dang weird." But the driver had driven on. That was fine with her. She left the truck in her normal parking spot and grabbed a water bottle from the back. The day was turning out to be a hot one already.

Turning the knob to the radio, she listened for the familiar buzz, but the radio light didn't even flash on. She forgot to charge the radio unit in all the commotion the night before between the horse and Emma's place.

Sherri closed her eyes and bowed her head. What was she doing? She tucked her phone in her pocket and clipped the fanny pack around her waist. Already a trickle of sweat made its way down the small of her back and under her shirt tucked into her jeans.

Locking the doors, she turned at the sound of a different truck pulling into the parking area. She smiled and approached the tinted window as the rig moved onto the gravel. Closing the trail would be easier, if she just tamped down any visitors from the get-go.

The truck revved its engine and accelerated from the curve. Tires spinning, the front bumper narrowly missed her shin as she jumped out of its path.

The truck rammed into the bed of her rig. Metal crunched, the sound reverberating through the trees and deafening all other sounds. Even her pulse pounding in her ears.

Glass tinkled onto the gravelly ground.

Staring for the briefest of seconds as reality crashed around her, Sherri accepted that she wasn't just afraid of fire. She was terrified of whoever had just intentionally crammed her truck into the forest boundaries.

Sherri couldn't get to her rig. The force of the larger Dodge had propelled her smaller Nissan through the parking space and into the log barrier set up at the trail head. Whoever it was in that cab they weren't there to help her out.

There was no time to hang out and ask what they were doing. Sherri had to get out of there immediately. Without over-thinking, Sherri spun, running toward the trail.

She skidded to a stop when the truck door opened and the man from the bar where she'd met Kyle – Guy, if she remembered right - staggered out. He shook his head, holding onto the door as he regained his bearings. He scanned the area, staring at her truck like she might have gotten back inside when he wasn't looking.

The barrier was crushed in, partially hanging over the packed down dirt of the trail on the other side of her truck.

Guy spotted her and tensed. His quiet voice carried across the short distance. "You're going to wish I hadn't missed when I get ahold of you."

Was he threatening her? Why would he want to hurt Sherri? What had she done?

Sherri edged further around the accident, trying to get out of Guy's range. He'd easily catch her, if she ran down the road. She wasn't that fast, unless she took to the trails and non-traveled paths of the forest. Not many could keep up with her in that regard. She might not be in great physical shape, but she understood the forest better than most.

Guy's wiry size would overcome her without any problems. But his tennis shoes wouldn't support his ankles well, if she led him down the mountain. Her boots were extremely supportive.

She'd have to count on that small bit of confidence to do anything about saving herself. There was no chance to call for help. The radio was out and her phone wasn't handy. Not when she had seconds to get out of there.

She watched his eyes shift as he still continued trying to gather his control. His lips thinned further and he ducked his head, his shoulders tight.

The crazy man was going to charge her like a bull.

Backing up further, she gauged the slope of the ground with her heels as she moved. Her boot slanted as the gravelly surface of the ground gave way.

Glinting in his eye warned her of his impending impetus forward.

He jerked toward Sherri and she whirled, slipping through the break in the fence and darting over the side of the mountain. Fortunately, she'd been that way multiple times since she'd moved back and she could say, fairly confidently, that she was headed toward Jonesy's Acres. At least in a general direction. She had a valley and then another ridge to get over before she was in range on foot.

Guy crashed and snapped multiple branches and other limbs behind her as he followed, spurring her on.

Maybe she was scared of more than just fire…

She slipped on dry, loose brush and dirt, propelling quickly downward. Even with her arms

273

out, she couldn't grasp any roots or low hanging branches for additional support.

Her legs hurt and she stumbled as a rotten log gave way under her weight. Pushing off the slanted ground, she rushed faster, the sounds of her pursuer closer and louder – his breathing coming in harder spurts than her own.

She hit the valley of the mountainside and leaned into the climb to get over the slight rise of the ridge before the final drop down toward the large section of land.

As Sherri dug in, lengthening her stride, the crashing behind her lessened until it stopped.

Don't look back. Don't look back. It's a trap. She glanced behind her, slowing down when the man didn't pop up in her line of sight. Where did he go? She turned to search for him. She wouldn't be caught unawares and there was no way he'd gotten ahead of her. Not on that steep of a rise. He'd been puffing like a heavy smoker.

Movement from a stand of Tamaracks caught her attention and she crouched down. He had something which flashed in the dim shadows of the forest, flickering orange and white.

"No! Stop!" She stood; arm outstretched as if she could compel him to stop building the fire in the crux of a very old tree.

He glanced at her; the fire already set.

Then he stood, tilting his head back and studying her through slanted eyes. "You'll come with me or I'll catch you down by the field. There's more than one way to flush a hare." He turned and climbed up the side of the hill, using the trees and brush to aid his climb.

After he reached halfway up and was far enough away to not be a problem, Sherri rushed from her spot above the valley floor and sprinted up the hill to the small fire which spread quickly.

No. No no no no no. No fire. Oh crap, the fire. She had to go near it. She had to actually be up close to it. Goosebumps scattered over her arms and up her neck and not because she was cold.

She couldn't breathe, overwhelmed by the exertion in the early heat of the summer day and her overwhelming fear of flames. Her pulse was erratic, but she'd have to worry about that later.

Gritting her teeth, she stamped at the fire eating at the edges of a growing circle.

Sherri whimpered.

Dry twigs and leaves succumbed to the hungry tongue of the flames. She scooped dirt onto some of the orange flames to smother it, but they ate at the dry foliage mixed in with the dirt. She backed up as her attempts to kill the fire only fueled its angry appetite.

Nothing she did was working.

The flames spread up the crackly bark of the old, drought weakened tree, catching hold and devouring the hair-like moss with increasing intensity.

Before her the fire grew from a small threat to a priority she couldn't get under control. She didn't know how. She couldn't even blame her crippling fear to its overabundant vigor.

Whipping her cell phone out, she dialed her boss's number and turned to run back up the hill away from the parking lot.

Guy had warned her. He'd promised to be waiting for her. She couldn't go around the fire – even if she wanted to.

She had to take her chances running from it.

Puffing hard as she crawled up the side of the hill, she slowed while her phone rang. And rang.

His voicemail came up. She gasped for air as she spoke, not taking the chance to stop. "Barry! Someone just. Started a fire. On purpose. I'm on the. Beaver. Ridge. Headed toward Jonesy's. Acres. Ruined the truck." Hanging up, she tried to regulate her breathing, but the adrenaline coursing through her messed with any semblance of control she wanted to pretend to have.

Smoke curled up the mountainside, swirling between the brush and the ferns littering the forest floor. Sherri coughed, searching for a break in the trees twenty feet above her. She had to get through them and start her mad dash down the other side.

Fingers clenched around the phone, she debated who to call. Best bet would be Kyle, but he didn't have a cell. Cyan? She dialed her best friend's number, stopping her scramble up for a second to press send. She then lunged forward, shoving her hands between the branches to get through the mass of thick trees.

She didn't want to need anyone. She had to save herself, but she needed help putting out the fire. She could admit that much.

Glancing back, she held in a sob at the sight of the flames moving quickly through the dry underbrush and seeming to leap from tree top to tree top with the slight breeze cresting over the canopy.

Cyan answered on the third ring.

"Cyan!" Sherri screamed; her voice already hoarse from the smoke-tinged air. "Beaver Ridge is on fire. Some guy chased me and started a forest fire. Get help. I don't know who to call. We haven't covered this in training yet." She hadn't covered much of anything except basic protocols. Being understaffed didn't help anyone.

"I'll make some calls. Where are you? Are you okay?" Cyan's breathlessness relieved Sherri.

She wasn't overreacting. Her friend took her seriously. Not that Sherri expected anything less, but with heat mounting behind her and a mad man potentially in front of her... Sherri didn't know what part of her reality had changed and what hadn't.

"I'm okay. I'm trying to get ahead of the fire. It's heading straight for Jonesy's place. Warn them. I'll be fine." She knelt down for a moment, her legs cramping and she leaned against the trunk of a small pine, while she held onto the phone like her last link with the real world. "Thank you." Her whisper barely reached above a sigh. Of course, she'd be fine. She could get herself out of that. No big deal.

"Sherri! Get out of there. I'll see if I can send someone to get you." Cyan barely restrained her panic, her voice dropping in desperation. "Seriously, get safe. I don't want you to get hurt."

Sherri didn't answer as she hung up. She couldn't. Her throat was swelling and just swallowing was painful.

She could do it. She could save herself. It wasn't far. She didn't have far to go. All the uphill climbing was behind her.

She tucked her phone into her back pocket. Where did she go? Could she go directly down to the ranch? Would she make it? She hadn't been down that way. The last time she went down the hill to get to the ranch, she'd gone down at an angle.

From her limited vantage point, thick smoke covered her view behind her, back the way she came.

The way Guy had said he'd be waiting. Or wait, had he said something about waiting for her down the hill away from him?

Vertigo sent her on a dizzying spin.

Trees faded as more smoke filled the air around her. She covered her mouth and nose, coughing as she staggered down the hill, tripping and tumbling down the rocky face.

How was it possible she'd entered her own personal hell?

Chapter 16

Kyle

Kyle recognized the truck that passed by the ranch mid-morning. He gritted his teeth as he finished rounding the barn from mounting his horse. He glared at Guy's rig as it sped past.

Nudging the horse with his knee, Kyle shook his head. He had to accept the fact that he wasn't everyone's hero. Since he'd started spending more time with Sherri, he hadn't been able to follow Guy on his night time forays into bars. And after he'd promised the guy he'd be there, watching him.

If he didn't do something to keep Guy in line, he'd think he'd scared Kyle off the night he got up in Kyle's face while Kyle was out with Sherri. Guy thinking he had any upper hand over Kyle was unacceptable.

Turning around the edge of the ranch, Kyle held the Arabian to a slow walk. He'd never named the horse, never cared enough to. He hadn't even asked the owner of the ranch what her name was. She was a gorgeous animal, but Kyle didn't allow himself to develop an attachment to her. She wasn't his.

Neither was Sherri, but he'd grown so attached to her over the last month or so, he didn't think he could detach himself easily. Kyle would have to humble himself and own up to Jareth that Kyle finally understood how fast Jareth had fallen for Cyan – even though they were complete opposites.

When a man knows, he knows. And even though Kyle didn't want to commit to anything hasty or permanent just yet, he knew.

Sherri was the girl he wanted in his life for as long as he could keep her there.

Bugs and all.

Would he lose everyone's respect, if he fell for a vegan bug collector? Did he care? Sherri had so many great qualities. Kyle would be an idiot to let her out of his life.

He was just smart enough to realize that. He couldn't wait to see her again.

The perimeter passed under the hooves of his ride smoothly. Nate had been so worried about the burn line; he'd had them double the width and raise the height of the fences with chicken wire to prevent large burning debris from floating or falling over the line.

Nate had thought of everything. If the field caught fire, the flames would spread faster than fog on a window and it would destroy the ranch.

A ranch he didn't own.

Kyle reached the far corner of the property; near the butterfly pond he'd taken Sherri to. Why couldn't he get his mind off her?

A whistle in the distance drew him from his thoughts and he adjusted his hat to see better.

Nate rode toward him at a full-on gallop. He drew up to Kyle, reining his horse in tight and then moving it in a circle to cool down. "Sherri's in trouble." Nate pointed over the hill at the edge of the fencing. "There's a fire coming this way. I just reported it to the fire patrol and we're getting some hoses out to get ready. I don't know where she is, but it's somewhere in the woods." He nodded into the forest. Sweat already beaded on his forehead and neck.

Panic welled in Kyle, but rather than spurn him into chaos, he calmed into a controlled stillness. "She's out there? Can she get out?" He searched the trees for the impossible sign of her running toward him. "Is she on a horse?"

"Cyan isn't sure. But some guy chased after her and then started the fire. Sherri didn't say who it was, but she said he's waiting for her. So, she's not going back to her truck. If she's smart, she'll head this way. Then we can watch for her and get her to safety." He pulled his horse a few feet away, wheeling around to face Kyle once more.

A guy chased after her. If she'd been up in the woods past Jonesys, then she'd been up at the trailheads where Guy had been headed. Why hadn't Kyle followed after him when he'd seen him?

Above the tree line, white smoke marred the otherwise flawless blue sky. Spreading across the blue expanse gave away the presence of a strong wind higher and higher up. The breeze around them suggested the wind was stronger at the higher altitudes.

"I need to find her." Kyle choked down the worry threatening to consume him. He didn't have any other choice. His entire being ached to rescue her.

"I can't help you, Kyle. I'm sorry. I have too much to do to protect this place. Good luck. Stay safe and get that girl." Nate nodded again, tapping the horse's flank with his boot. The large animal bolted, as if he sensed the urgency in the moment.

Nate didn't say it, but he needed help, yet he'd never put Kyle in the position to choose and Kyle knew it.

Plus, Nate would never put a person's life below the well-being of material objects. He wanted Kyle to do what he had to do so Nate could focus on the ranch.

If what Sherri had said about the fire danger in that area was correct, Kyle hoped she got out of there fast. The flames would move speedily with the breeze coming from the west.

He looked back at the ranch. Did he help with the fire protection or did he go after Sherri? Of course, he would find her and help her. Of course, he couldn't conceivably consider anything else. Not when his heart longed to have her in his arms again, safe and sound.

He had no doubt in his mind the man was Guy. Didn't it add up? Kyle didn't realize Sherri had gone up to the ridge that morning, but it made sense. Guy wasn't a nature fan.

Guy had followed her. Did Kyle go after him or did he rush to Sherri? Was she safe enough to reach the ranch soon?

Why was he even debating what to do? He'd go after Sherri, but Nate needed him, too. Guilt ate at him even as he spurred his horse through a break in the fencing and up a trail onto the mountainside.

He'd make sure he got back to help with the ranch in time. He would.

Because if he didn't make it, then that meant he hadn't found Sherri in time.

~~~

Kyle adjusted the bandana he'd tied around his face. The smoke had grown thicker the higher he'd climbed. If he didn't turn back, he'd endanger the horse. He climbed off the Arabian and smacked her rear-end with a "heeyah" to send her home. She trotted down the nearest trail toward the ranch. Kyle just hoped it wasn't too late.

He turned back to the wall of smoke that hid a crackling hot mess behind its veil of white. His eyes watered and his mouth filled with a metallic taste. He couldn't go closer; the heat was too intense. He'd been all along the line of fire as it crawled closer toward the ranch.

A helicopter passed overhead with a bucket hanging from its skids. It disappeared into the smoke cover, leaving Kyle to separate the sounds of the fire ravaging the woods and the blades chopping through the air.

When did he admit defeat? When did he let his heart know there wasn't any hope? Did he accept the loss?

But he couldn't give up yet. He had to find her. Maybe he'd missed her on one of his passes. She was probably sitting at the ranch right that moment, drinking ice cold water and reporting the incident to the police.

A burning tree crashed through the forest and the loud whinny of a horse pulled Kyle that direction.

He stepped over the logs and bushes teeming with escaping bugs and creatures. A doe shot across his field of view as he reached the fallen burning mass.

The Arabian he'd sent away had gotten stuck between tightly growing brush and the flaming tree. Her eyes rolled; the whites larger than the pupils. She blew, her lips moving. She reared from him, as if he was another threat she couldn't escape from.

Kyle climbed through the leaves and branches of the brush, stomping them down and pushing them to the sides and reaching out his hands to calm the horse. "Sh. Come on. Let's get out of here. I bet she's down at the ranch. Nate probably has her and they're all fine." His muttering calmed the horse enough he grabbed her free hanging reins. "Let's go." He tugged her through the small hole in the bushes, desperate to free her from the trap. "I didn't think before sending you off, lady, I'm sorry."

Lady. He liked that. She'd be Lady. Maybe he could let himself get a little more attached to the people and things in his life. They had a great job there at the ranch and there was no reason why he wouldn't get to stay on a little longer.

He tugged harder, pulling Lady's head down under branches and low bending snags. She didn't protest as he pulled her further from the heat, down the mountain.

With each step away from the fire, Kyle's hopes crumbled a little more. Was he being stupid? Was he abandoning Sherri to the inferno raging across the forest?

Was he ever going to find her or had he lost what he'd just realized he needed?

Chapter 17

Sherri

Sherri didn't remember falling. She lifted her head from the hot ground. Her fingers by her face were red with blood. Throbbing pain just above her eyebrow pulsed frantically. Her cheek rubbed intimately with dirty bark and heat tamped down all around her. She rolled to her back, desperate to get her bearings.

The fire was closing in.

Standing on wobbly legs, she coughed through a dry throat. Crackling and smoke surrounded her, overwhelming her senses.

She could do it. She could do it. She had to get out of there. She could do it. She had to.

The ground beneath her feet slanted to the right. Down. She just had to get down. If she could just get down, she'd be able to get on the ranch land.

She didn't even care how she got down. She slid on loose needles on her butt most of the way, finally standing where she could run on flat land.

Reaching the corner of the land furthest from the ranch, she stopped to look for a way through.

The fire line ditch had been expanded further and the fencing ran even higher. She'd never get over the high wire or crawl under the low poles.

She fell to her knees in the dry dirt, sobs ripping from her raw throat. Lacing her fingers over the loops of the fencing, she hung her head and closed her eyes. She had to get somewhere safe. But where?

Maybe she wasn't going to be able to do this on her own.

Under her arm, she watched the fire reach the line about fifty feet from where she knelt, burning and trying to get over the dirt. She scrabbled to her feet, gasping for air that wasn't the pure Montana air she took for granted.

A tree with flames burning high into the sky fell across the dirt ditch and smashed through the fence.

Fire grabbed hold of the wheat field and spread fast.

Sherri stumbled backward. She didn't have many options. She needed to find water. Whether she thought she could do it or not, if she wanted to live, she had to try. There wasn't another soul around to help her, anyway.

If was her… or the fire.

A tick crept down her arm. Its legs maneuvered over the lines of her shirt. She brushed it off, sad it wouldn't make it.

How many bugs and wild animals were dead because of Guy? The butterfly retreat popped in her mind and she turned. She had nothing else to head towards. Not with the minimal energy she had. She'd never make it to the road.

The trail seemed to stretch forever with fire eating up the ground behind her, faster and faster.

She picked up her feet, but really only succeeded in shuffling a little faster. Fine, she'd take it. She just wanted to get to the water. She needed to. How had she gotten so tired? How far had she really come?

Why hadn't Cyan sent anyone to help her? The ranch was under attack from the flames and Sherri didn't blame the ranch hands for working on saving the ranch. She understood.

She just wanted to see Kyle one more time before she died.

And she would die. She couldn't save herself. She could see that now. Even the helicopters weren't coming to that side of the fire. They appeared to be working on the fire closest to the road, probably to keep it from town and the reservation.

No, no one was coming.

She couldn't do it. Sherri gripped her fingers into her palms. She pumped her arms harder, gasping and whimpering as she struggled toward the clearing.

Almost there. Twenty feet. Fifteen. She could do it. Keep going. Keep. Going. Ten.

Five feet to go and Sherri reached the pond. Her skin stung as the heat closed in around her.

With little thought, Sherri fell into the chilly water fully clothed. The difference in temperatures took her breath away and she came up gasping. Quickly she relowered her body under the water, tucking her knees to her chest. She pulled her outer shirt off to wrap around her face. The rest of her had to fit under the water, yet she still had to be able to breathe.

She curled the shirt and placed it on her face, leaving a small hole for air to get through and then leaned back, submerging everything up to the edges of the shirt.

Panic threatened to drown her. Holding it at bay, she focused. Or tried to focus. But focus on what? She didn't know how long she had to be under there. She didn't know the rate of evaporation or even the intensity of the burn. She didn't know anything. If she'd had more time...

Was there a chance that she could still save herself?

Eyes closed shut and encased in a watery prison that was surrounded by guards of inferno, Sherri could finally admit to herself that she really did need others. She needed Cyan and Rachiah. She needed her parents.

She needed Kyle. He made her laugh and was jealous when other guys talked to her which flattered her because he felt deeply enough for that. He wasn't controlling and didn't have any problem laughing at himself when he made a mistake. They hadn't known each other a long time, but she'd known him long enough to know that she wanted him in her life a lot longer – if not indefinitely.

Dang it, that stung. Admitting that she needed *anyone*. But the realization didn't sting half as much as realizing that she might die there… in that chilly water… alone.

If she'd had more time, maybe she could've…

No, not even then. Because of some random nut job, she hadn't been able to warn anyone with enough time. She hadn't had enough time to tell anyone she loved them. That stark reality cut deeper than any burn on her hands and face.

But with the level of drought and stressed plant life, would there have been an adequate amount of time? How long would it have been? Was anyone even fighting the fire?

Sherri hadn't seen any signs of life. Even the butterflies of the clearing were absent as she'd clattered through their home.

The surface of the water warmed around her.

Sherri didn't dare bring her face out of the water to check. She dipped lower to drench the shirt material more as it dried under intense heat.

Under her legs, cool water moved across the backs of her jeans. Hadn't Kyle said the pond was fed by an underground stream? Maybe it would be just enough to keep the water from getting too warm and keep it refilled enough to fight the evaporation rate.

How long would she be there? Would anyone find her? Was anyone looking for her?

Would she see Kyle or Cyan or Rachiah ever again?

Too many doubts and uncertaintiesd swelled inside her heart and she longed to scream. Instead she breathed scorching air through the small opening and hoped she didn't pass out.

And drown.

Chapter 18

Kyle

Grabbing a bucket when he got back to the ranch, Kyle sprinted around the south end of the barn and joined the line at the trough to funnel water to the fire line.

While swinging the bucket, he searched the crowd for anyone who knew who Sherri was.

Soot covering his face, Jareth rushed by.

Kyle clutched his brother's sleeve. "Jareth, have you seen Sherri? Is she inside?"

Jareth shook his head, pushing his hat off his sweating forehead. "Nah, Cyan keeps calling for her, but we don't have time to search for her because Nate said you were. The field caught on fire on the only side of the field we weren't on. You better find Sherri. I'd hate to be the one to tell Cyan something happened to her best friend." Jareth's eyes widened as he looked past Kyle's shoulder. "Holy crap, I haven't seen that bastard in a long time."

Kyle turned, narrowing his gaze. Guy stood beside his truck, arms crossed and a smirk smudging his face.

Approaching at a slow swagger that sped up into a near-sprint, Kyle and Jareth came at Guy like a couple of jaguars, cautious but hungry. Kyle jerked his chin up, his eyes wild. "What are you doing here?"

Tilting his head toward the flames, Guy pretended to yawn. "I saw the fire and thought I'd come see what was going on. Looks like you have a bit of a problem." He cocked his eyebrow, like he hadn't done anything wrong.

Where was she? Just the thought of what Sherri was probably going through curled Kyle's lip. He lunged forward, wrapping his fingers in the upper material of Guy's shirt. Yanking the weasel toward him, he forced Guy onto his tiptoes.

Lips tight and teeth clenched, Kyle growled. "Where is she?"

As he realized who Kyle spoke about, Guy's eyes grew round. "That chick? She's not back?" He searched what he could, but his vantage point was tiny and hard to maneuver with the hold Kyle had him in. "She should've been back by now. I didn't wreck her truck that bad." His voice turned into a whine. "Seriously, Darby, I didn't mean to get her hurt. I thought for sure she'd make it down here by now. I just wanted—"

Kyle gave him a little shake. "You started the fire, right?" He didn't acknowledge the firefighters and fire marshal who had walked up behind them. He just needed witnesses and he'd take them in anyone he thought was viable.

Guy whimpered.

Kyle shook him again, repeating louder. "You did the fire, right? Trying to hurt Sherri?"

Nodding, Guy shuddered. "Yes, yes, I did it. I was just trying to get her attention." His fingers scrabbled at Kyle's clenched fists as he tried to loosen the hold.

Kyle dropped him, looking over his head to the officials and nodding his head. He turned to Jareth. "I need to find her. I can't just wait here."

"You're going to have to wait, brother. The fire is too high. You can't go out there." Jareth clapped his hand on the upper part of Kyle's arm. His grim expression didn't help Kyle's spiraling despair. He'd given up too soon. He could've saved her. She was out there *still*. But where? Where was she?

A shout in the distance drew their attention. The fire had spread across the prairie, making any attempts at extinguishing it next to impossible. The fire ate at the ground, driven relentlessly by the wind and dry grasses.

The rancher-style home and barn lay directly in its path.

"Grab more buckets!" Nate's shout reached the group over the wind that had suddenly picked up faster and the panicked neighing. "Get to the barn."

Kyle bent at the waist, swooping up his dropped water bucket and sprinting toward the barn. He had to release the horses. Lady was already out. She huddled against the only fence that hadn't been attacked by flames. Kyle reached the doors as men screamed from the far side that the roof had caught on fire.

Running inside, he unlocked the stall doors and chased the horses out of the building. Clapping his hands, he searched every stall for any strays. Even as the barn filled with smoke, he couldn't take the chance that even one of the animals would be left behind.

As soon as the stalls were checked, Kyle locked the doors behind him so nothing would get back inside and breathed the fresher air with a desperate gulp.

Even with all the men organized and fighting the flames, the wind proved to be too much and the house caught fire as well. Its golden-brown logs charred and blackened while the glass burst as the heat reached it.

The firefighters pulled everyone to the side and made them stay out of the way as they fought to keep the fire contained since the log home burned too hot and fast.

Kyle's cousins slumped against the wooden logs of the fence, defeat belaboring their expressions. The entire Montana Trail group had lost more than their job site there. They somehow had lost all hope for their future.

Too much loss for that day compounded itself into more loss than a decade could support.

"We lost the whole place. Mr. Jonesy won't be happy." Nate moved up beside him, eyes teary and blood shot. "Did you find Sherri?"

"He's insured though, right?" Jareth moved up beside Nate. Leaned across to Kyle and looked around. "Did you find Sherri?"

Kyle shook his head and swallowed hard. His answer was more a croak. "No. I tried. I couldn't find her. It's not like she could hide in some water and —" He snapped his head up.

Could she have made it to the butterfly pond? Could she be out there waiting for someone to save her?

Him?

He couldn't risk the lives of any of the horses. Breaking into a run, he hollered over his shoulder. "Call nine-one-one, Jareth. I think I know where Sherri is."

With the fire raging closer to the mountain range and pulling back from the edge of the woods, maybe the small clearing had fared better than the ranch or the surrounding fields.

Did he have enough time or had he wasted every second he had working on a ranch no one had been able to save?

He pushed his guilt to the side until he could mull it over later. If he could save her, he might be able to save himself some pain later.

Heat pulsated off the rolling waves of fire, slapping him with the full-frontal abuse it could manage from only a hundred feet away.

From that angle, he'd never get in. Stomping through the remains of the cremated field, Kyle adjusted his sweat-dampened bandana up over his nose. He'd go around, see if there was a break in the flames and heat. No one had seen her and the fire had crossed the road. All of Clearwater County would be worried about the fire at this point. Hopefully, they were able to contain it to the area immediately around Taylor Falls.

As long as Kyle didn't think too hard, he wouldn't have to face the glaring truth that his vigilantism was the reason Guy had started the fire, was the reason Sherri was in danger – if even still alive.

The blame belonged to Kyle. Which went to prove the saying that no good deed goes unpunished.

Another helicopter hovered above him then dipped and pushed its bucket closer to the clearing Kyle headed for. Stopping and making as if to lower the bucket, the helicopter halted the lowering and angled up at a slant, then flew to the right, disappearing over the fields to get closer to the river that ran parallel to the town.

Kyle tromped closer to the clearing. Had they seen something? Could she be there? The heat was too high and Kyle stopped. He'd never get past the heat barrier.

If he couldn't get in, how would Sherri ever survive inside?

The helicopter returned, its bucket swaying back and dropping water behind it. Stopping, the helicopter didn't go past the area it'd hovered before. Kyle backed up to see better.

The bucket tipped, pouring its contents as the helicopter moved. The pilot angled backwards, spilling the water over the less burning smaller trees as if to create a path for Kyle. The heat dissipated, but not enough for Kyle to get inside. With only the one chopper working with the water, the heat evaporated the water faster than he could get it.

Chopping sounds from the opposite direction made Kyle turn. Another helicopter zoomed overhead, its bucket full and ready to tip. The first helicopter returned for more water and the second spread its offering. The flames dissipated more, the heat turning down a few notches.

While the second continued dropping its water, the first made progress getting that way.

Spray from the steam soaked Kyle, cooling him even for a moment.

All of the flames on the clearing perimeter closest to him fell back, revealing blackened corpses of fallen and scorched trees and bushes.

Kyle didn't wait for the fire to return. He kicked hard, lifting his knees and running as fast as possible through the break in the fire to the clearing.

Ash and scarred debris littered the surface of the pond. A long black branch had fallen into the water, protruding from the edge. In the center of the pond, an oddly shaped island the size of a shoe floated just at the water surface.

Kyle held his breath. He didn't even stop at the edge, but plunged into the luke warm waters. The temperature threw him off. Normally the waters he was waist deep in were icy cold.

He didn't hesitate as he bent down and wrapped his arms around Sherri's body, claiming her as his. Kyle didn't wait to find out if she was dead or alive.

They didn't have time. He had to get her out of there before the fire reclaimed the trail the choppers had created. The water the helicopters had dropped wouldn't hold the torrential flames at bay for long.

Kyle lifted her soaking body from the water and she clung to him, spluttering and coughing as he rose from the pond bed. He croaked past impending tears at the evidence she was still alive. "Hang on, Sherri. I'll get you out of here." He uttered a prayer that he could get help to rescue them both and allowed the relief that she was still alive flood him, releasing the band around his chest and allowing him to breathe better. To hope again.

He tightened his arms around her, but she pushed from him. "I can stand."

Eyeing her with suspicion like she might fall over at any second, Kyle set her on her feet and pulled on her arm. "Let's get out of here." The dark brown of her shirt lightened around the edges as it dried in the intensifying heat. She focused on the ground in front of her, not meeting his gaze as her hair dripped around her face. They took off at a jog, running through the steaming and smoking sections of the previously dampened area.

He didn't relent, pushing Sherri at full speed until they reached the safety of the already-burned fields. The heat there wasn't as hot as it beat down on them from the sun and sideways from the fire.

Slowing, Kyle didn't wait until they'd fully stopped before pulling Sherri into his arms. He rocked back and forth; his eyes closed.

The immense emotion overwhelming him took his voice and all he could do for a moment was just hold her. Just keep her in that moment, safe in his arms.

She clung to the backs of his arms. Her legs bent and then suddenly her weight dropped and unprepared, Kyle sank to the ground with her rather than drop her.

She'd passed out and judging by the red welts on her face and hands, she still wasn't safe. How foolish to think that getting her out of the immediate flames was enough to protect her from harm.

His adrenaline abating, Kyle struggled to his feet, scooping her into his arms again. He'd get her safe, if it killed him.

The next hundred yards stretched before him like miles with the heat bearing down on all sides. He was already exhausted, facing the rescue had drained his adrenaline. Once he reached the driveway, he fell to his knees, hollering for help from anyone who would give it. His raspy voice only half as loud as normal.

The smoke inhalation had made his throat swell. He swallowed to call for more help.

The man watching over Guy rushed to Kyle's side. He checked Sherri's pulse and lifted his fingers to his lips, emitting a piercing whistle. Another fireman dropped a bucket he worked at the well and ran over to help with Sherri. They stretched her out and stabilized her neck on Kyle's lap.

He tried not to look like he might cry as he asked, "Is she going to be alright?" He couldn't lose her. He needed her. Kyle just hadn't realized how much until right then.

"I don't know. We're going to call an ambulance. Just hang on." The grim set to the firefighter's lips chilled Kyle in the sweltering heat.

What if she didn't make it?

There was no doubt that Guy had gone out there to make a point with Sherri to Kyle. He wanted to get Sherri and pay Kyle back for embarrassing him. Kyle never thought he'd take it to such dangerous levels.

Guy's fire could have killed Sherri, any of the ranchers, and who knew who else from town? The fire wasn't out yet and there still a lot of people in danger.

What if Kyle had lost the ranch, his job, and his girl all because he had to have revenge on something that had happened to his sister a long time ago?

Chapter 19

Sherri

Being pulled from the water wasn't as memorable as being cradled in Kyle's arms. Sherri's throat didn't want to let her breathe. She'd choked on smoke and coughed up water. Everything felt scorched and singed and achy and tight. Would she ever be pain free again?

Waking up in the hospital, Sherri hoped it was all a dream. Her throat burned and her lungs ached. If it was a dream, it'd been a nightmare. She tried to breathe in deeply but even with the oxygen tube stuck in her nose, she couldn't get as much air as she wanted.

No one came to visit. She stayed in the hospital for a few days, but after they determined she would be okay, they released her. Clearing her for edema in the lungs and verifying all her burns were only second-degree left Sherri feeling like she'd passed a solid checklist of what she needed to hit before being let go.

Why hadn't she had any visitors? It was only a couple days, but Cyan, Rachiah, even Maverick would be welcome. Of course, Sherri was hoping for too much in wishing Kyle would show up, but she still wanted to see him, even if it was too much.

Standing at her place in the doorway after paying for a cab left her bereft and more isolated than even half-drowning in that pond.

Had Tommy been okay? Would anyone even miss her, if she died? Kyle had disappeared after carrying her somewhere. She didn't remember much of anything.

She sat on her patio, not willing to cram herself and her nerves into the small, lonely home. Even her roommate was missing.

The pain was starting to come back, ripping under her skin and along the lines of her muscles. She fumbled in her bag for the small orange bottle of medication the hospital had given her. After popping a couple more pills without a drink of water, she sank to the top step of the patio in front of the silent house.

Wrapping her bandaged arms around her knees, she brushed her hair off her forehead. Singed ends curled tightly around her fingers. She didn't allow herself to cry. She couldn't.

But the tears still escaped. She had forced her tears back all that time. Even the sobbing hadn't been real crying, just a way to release her pent-up fear.

Four days and no one had come looking for her. No one. Not even Cyan.

The only thing that would keep Cyan away from Sherri was if Cyan herself was dead. Real dread flooded Sherri's heart. Cyan. Had Cyan died in the fire? Had something happened?

All the hospital staff had talked about was the fire. It still raged on, even now, mostly burning north and to the west on National forest land. But the danger was still there it would shift with the winds and head toward Taylor Falls and Colby.

The rumble of M.T.'s Bronco announced his arrival, but Sherri didn't look up. She stared at the brown dry edges of the greenish blades of grass. Blistered, her hands ached and she didn't pick at the grass as she normally would have.

Before.

Even the orange and red burning flames along the horizon didn't warrant more than a passing glance. She'd been up close and personal with those flames. She didn't want to see more of them then absolutely necessary. A smokey haze tinged the air, hurting Sherri's throat more fully than when she was in the car or at the hospital.

M.T. left his rig running. He rounded the front with urgency hardening his strong jaw and the normal tenderness in his eyes. "Sherri, where have you been? We're evacuating the reservation. You need to —" He stopped feet from her, taking in her appearance. "Holy crap, Sherri. What happened?" He bent and brushed her hair from her face.

Sherri swallowed, her throat tight and still painful. She whispered, "I need to see Kyle." She had to see him. He knew what she'd been through, but not only that, he'd saved her. He'd been there. He'd been there when she needed him. He'd come for her when no one else had. If what she remembered about the rescue, the small amount that she did, then he'd come for even when the flames burned higher than him.

M.T.'s face stiffened. His long hair moved with him as he pulled from her. "Did he do this to you?"

Sherri stood on aching legs. She lifted her chin. "M.T., that's not what happened. He pulled me out of the fire. I can't call the taxi service from Colby. Not if they're evacuating. Can you get me to Kyle? He's probably at the Bella Acres. He saved me." Too many words. Her throat closed up again and she shook her head instead of continuing.

One hand at her throat, she held up a finger for him to wait and ran inside. She needed Tommy. She couldn't leave him in case the res burned down.

She grabbed Tommy in his traveling case and looked once at her place. If she didn't see her stuff, she wouldn't be heart-broken. She hadn't been alive long enough to create a lasting bond with anything. But now, thanks to Kyle, she had a chance at more time to develop relationships with more people, be more to more people.

Need more.

She had to tell him how much he meant to her. Even if they weren't ready for *I love you*, at least they would have the time to find out.

M.T. helped her up into the cab of his rig and closed the door. He climbed in beside her in the driver's seaet and backed out of the drive. After a moment, as he drove them from the reservation, he spoke cautiously, "*He* saved you?"

She nodded, but couldn't speak. She clutched her hand to her throat, the pain holding her words in. Rolling down her window, she spit the excess saliva out of her mouth that she couldn't swallow.

"Maybe I owe him more than jealousy." He pulled over to the side of the road and turned toward her. He held up his hand, his dark eyes watching her. "I know you can't speak, which is perfect for me. You always shut me down before I even get started."

M.T. studied her, his smile tender but sad. "I love you. You know I do. I always have. But I'm not stupid. I've seen the way you look at this guy. If you care about him," he swallowed, "love him, then I'll back off. I just want you to be happy. But if you don't care about him, tell me now. I won't give up, if I think there's the smallest chance you could care for me."

Grasping the moment to really see him, not just as a brother or a constant fixture in her life, she could honestly say everything about him entranced her. She'd grown accustomed to M.T. being around but where his eyes were dark, she wanted to see blue and where his black hair hung long, she wanted to see the shorter hair peaking from under a cowboy hat.

She scrunched her nose, blinking back bittersweet tears, and whispered. "I love him." Immediately, she slapped her hand over her mouth. What had she said? How could she say that? It couldn't be true.

Maybe he hadn't heard. Her pride hoped that was true.

She couldn't *love* Kyle. She wasn't supposed to love anyone.

Insects were her choice, they didn't hurt you and they were consistent, reliable, predictable. Even though Sherri's childhood had been relatively boring, she'd been around Cyan and Rachiah long enough to see that men could hurt you or leave you, leaving you with your heart ripped out and your soul despairing.

A woman was better off not needing a man. Not wanting a man.

But Sherri had already accepted that she needed Kyle. Was it such a stretch that she could love him, too? How could she not accept that when she'd just bared her feelings to Maverick, the last man she would ever do expose her vulnerabilities of the heart to. Not when they could potentially hurt him.

"You love him? You barely know him." M.T. snorted in disgust, turning angrily to the steering wheel and pulling onto the road.

Did Sherri know Kyle enough to love him? How much did she need to know? He'd saved her twice and hadn't taken advantage of her either time – when he had more than enough opportunity. He teased her and made her laugh and he was jealous of her – he wanted her all to himself. None of those things were bad, though, and she couldn't reject the idea completely.

The horror at her sudden admission melted away. She could get used to the idea of loving him. Just because she felt the way she did, didn't mean she had to marry him that day. She could do what Cyan had done and take her time.

After the too-close experience with the fire, Sherri doubted she'd take *too* long. She wanted happiness and stability and she didn't want to come home to an empty house by herself again.

Mostly she wanted to be around someone who drove her crazy. She didn't want safe, vanilla feelings. She wanted the crazy stirrings inside her when she saw him and the safety of just being around him.

Like when she was with Kyle. But uncertainty swarmed her good feelings of self-discovery.

Would he even want her? Was he okay? Between Cyan, Rachiah, and Kyle, why hadn't anyone visited her in the last couple days?

The time to get to Nate's ranch passed in discomfort. His ranch was south of the reservation, so that area didn't look to be evacuating yet.

But with Montana neighborliness, more horses and stock than Nate normally had were rounded into the southern-most field where the creek was. Extra hay had been spread out along the fence line.

Her callousness toward M.T. slapped her in the face when she gave him more than just a cursory glance with fresh perspective. He was a good-looking man, was kind and considerate. He just wasn't for her.

She reached over and curled her fingers over his on the steering wheel when he stopped the rig at the house. She didn't have the words tell him what she was thinking, feeling, even regretting. She wasn't a normally mean person. She didn't want to hurt Maverick. But unfortunately, some things couldn't be helped.

M.T.'s shoulders lifted and dropped in a sigh. He shook his head and leaned back in his seat, not pulling away from her touch. He stared at her fingers on his. After a second he nodded. "I know." He patted her hand with his and then pushed her away. "I need to check the reservation for anymore stubborn residents." He nodded at her and looked out his window, turning completely away.

"I'm sorry." Her whisper was butterfly soft, but in the sudden silence of the truck, he heard. His tiny nod told her it was okay to get out.

She slid from the seat and grabbed her Tommy's cage. Closing the door felt like shutting away a part of her childhood. She had to have faith that he would find someone, someday. Because her finding happiness while he didn't just wasn't fair.

The steps to the deck rose before her with daunting steepness. Before that, she hadn't really noticed the angles and edges. But everything hurt and she didn't want to climb so much when she really didn't even want to move.

But the chance that Kyle was in there pushed her past her limits. She had to see him. Cyan, too.

The excruciating climb passed before she knew it and she took a breath before knocking on the door. She worried at her lower lip with her teeth. She couldn't talk. Honestly, she probably should be in bed resting with the burns on her hands, face, and neck. Not that she could stay with her bed. Sudden displacement slapped her in the face. She didn't have a home for the moment.

Guy had done that. Anger held her together. She refused to let him wound her further. He could take all of that away from her.

But she'd survived the fire. Not alone. But she'd survived it.

Her shoulders straightened. She had survived the fire. Even in the midst of the flames and the heat, she'd survived. Kyle had rescued her, but she'd made it. She'd gotten over her fear and taken the steps to stay alive.

She could do anything. She'd faced her biggest fear.

And won.

If Sherri could do that, she could talk to Kyle about what was going through her head and heart.

Doubt warred with her confidence. What was she doing? He'd never believe her when she said – or rather whispered – that she loved him. Maybe she'd pantomime it and he'd misunderstand. Or they could play Pictionary or something. Then she could save her pride.

She didn't have any way out of there to escape humility.

Even if she wanted to call someone else, she had no cell phone after jumping into the pond with everything in her pockets and no car. She had to go inside to make a call.

Who would help her?

Sucking in a deep breath, she knocked on the door again.

Another moment passed before the door opened.

Kyle stood on the other side, his eyes red-rimmed and downcast. "Yeah?" He looked up, his eyes growing wide as he recognized her. "Sherri!" He reached for her, careful when he touched her elbow and joined her on the deck. "Sherri, you're here. I called the hospital and they said you didn't make it." His voice cracked on the last two words and he adjusted his hat, his eyes bloodshot in the shadows.

Soot covered his face, dark in the creases around his eyes and by his nose. His flannel shirt had burn spots in it and his jeans were closer to black than blue. But he was refreshing. His blue eyes so clear, so concerned and relieved at the same time.

Sherri furrowed her brow, slightly shaking her head.

"Which hospital did you go to?" He rushed on, only waiting for her head movements. "I called Missoula. No? Colby, then?" At her nod, he grunted. "I should've called Colby. I – wow, your burns don't look as bad as they did on the ranch." He reached his fingers up like he meant to touch her cheek.

She turned to the side, wary of more pain on her already sensitive and blistered skin.

"It's okay, I won't hurt you." He dropped his hand. "I'm sorry. Are you okay?"

She shook her head, but reached out to reclaim his fingers with hers.

"Ah, I see. You can't talk. That's okay. Why don't you come inside? Everyone thinks you're dead – well, I told them you were because… well, I didn't think you made it." He slapped his leg. "They meant you hadn't made it to *their* hospital." He carefully wrapped his arm around her back. "Come on. I'll get you something to drink for your throat."

Sherri stopped him, releasing his fingers to put her hand on his arm. She shook her head and brushed her thumb over his chin. Her throat tightened further, leaving her breath more ragged.

Glancing down at their joined hands, she fought for just enough throat control to say, "I love you, Kyle." She grabbed her throat, wrinkling her nose and tucking her chin as she peeked at him through her lashes. "Too soon?"

"I can't… No, it's not too soon. But I don't want you to feel like you have to say that to me. I saved you, but that doesn't mean you owe me anything." Kyle stared at her, then hung his head. "This was all my fault. I've been after Guy for a long time to get even with him for doing to my sister what he tried to do to you. The fire. You. Everything is because I wouldn't leave it alone."

"Not. Fault." Sherri shook her head and closed her eyes, exhausted at the effort to talk and stand there. She needed to sit, to rest. But she needed to make him hear her more. "No. I. Love." But she couldn't finish. Her eyes closed halfway as she sagged forward.

Kyle's suspicion faded to wonder. "Really? You really feel that way?"

She nodded, embarrassed that her raw feelings had been lain out there like the burns on the backs of her hands and face.

He didn't say anything, just studied her, watched her. Like she had more to reveal.

Touching her arm, Kyle was soft at first and then applied more pressure. "I thought you were dead and I didn't get to tell you what I'd realized earlier. How much you mean to me." He brushed his knuckles over her hair and along her ear. "And now, here you are. Alive and I've been given a second chance. I'm so lucky." He leaned forward, brushing his lips across her sensitive lips. His whispered words breezed over her blistered skin. "I love you, too."

And it was like he released her pain, filling her instead with euphoria with his simple answer and she hadn't had to ask him to say something.

Her favorite thing about Kyle? He worked to protect her. She could handle that kind of affection. She could take care of herself, but he wouldn't *make* her do anything on her own.

She was free because her heart was unbridled, able to be and love as she wanted. Kyle gave that to her.

"Come on, the family will be so excited to see you." He opened the door and motioned her through. "We're just meeting for a family council. Nate was just about to announce something."

Sherri couldn't help but feel like her whole future had the potential to be in that room, at least with the man by her side.

She could handle that. She retrieved her tarantula from where she'd left him on the top of the steps and followed him indoors. He was treating her like a part of the family. Just how far would they be able to take their newfound feelings?

Hopefully, they had plenty of time to find out.

Chapter 20

Kyle

Sherri was there. Somehow, she'd gotten her spider and showed up at Nate's. She couldn't talk and Kyle didn't care. He'd get the answers from her when she could give them. He'd take whatever he could get. The last four days had been horrific as they'd fought fires and caught up on sleep in random places only to head right back out.

When he'd called the hospitals in Missoula and been told she didn't make it, he had returned to the fire fighting with a reckless abandon. His fury at her loss the only thing that made his loss capable of being coped with, worked with. He hadn't taken the time to face his loss. He couldn't. And now, he didn't really have to.

The family had gathered an hour ago. Everyone was exhausted and avoided the topic of Sherri because Kyle held up a hand when anyone asked. He hadn't had a chance to call any other hospital. Honestly, though, he hadn't known they had a facility in Colby that could handle burn victims.

None of that mattered, though, now. Nothing.

Sherri was alive and she walked inside with him. He had her.

She loved him. In light of the fire and the fact that he'd almost lost her, it didn't seem too soon. It didn't seem near soon enough. They had plenty to discover about each other, but thankfully, their time was open and they could prioritize what they wanted. For Kyle, his priority was going to be her.

He led the way to the kitchen where Nate sat at the head of the table with his head in his hands.

"Sherri!" Cyan's half-scream announced Sherri before anything else could. She rushed from behind the kitchen counter, a towel in her hands. She half-tackled Sherri before Kyle could stop her. Her pale skin attested to the loss she, too, had been feeling. "You're not dead. Oh my gosh, Sher, you're not dead." She pulled back, tears streaking her cheeks.

Sherri didn't seem to care. She dealt with any pain Cyan's touch might have caused. She accepted it.

But Kyle still stepped forward and gently moved Cyan's hands from Sherri's burned forearms. "She's pretty burned up and can't talk very well." But she'd said she loved him. That was talking perfectly, as far as he was concerned.

"Oh, sorry. Of course." Cyan jerked her hands back, staring at Sherri in wonder.

The rest of the people in the room exclaimed over her good fortune, but Sherri acknowledged them with a soft smile before she stared at her friend. Her whisper reached Cyan and Kyle. "Happened?"

Cyan wiped at her cheeks. "The fires are still burning. They can't find the guy who started the fire or chased you… and…" She glanced at the Montana Trails sitting around the room. "The Jonesy ranch is gone and so are three more along the northern edge of Clearwater." She glanced down, her hands clasped together at waist level.

"Jonesy's place didn't have full coverage." Nate's words broke through Kyle's mixed bitterness that they'd lost Guy and happiness at finding Sherri was alive.

Jareth groaned. "No. What does that mean?"

Emma's soft voice carried from an easy chair set up in the corner. "It means, we're responsible for the difference which comes to about fifty-thousand dollars. Since Nate was the foreman, we're taking it. You guys don't need to worry about any of it."

Cyan dropped her hands from Sherri and reached for Jareth's elbow. "I could ask my parents to help. They would give it to us." But her voice trailed off as the Montana Trail cousins lifted their chins in pride.

"Thanks, Cyan, but we can't take money like that. We need to figure out another way." Emma's sweet smile belied the worry in her twisting fingers as she worried at the blanket on her lap.

Nate met her gaze and then looked away sharply. "I can do it. We can figure something out."

"Nate, stop. We can't even cover basic medical for us. For me." Emma threw back the comforter on her frail appearing frame.

Stefanie stood; her hands braced on the table. "I'll work on the ranches, too. I can do that. I'm sick of working in town, Nate. I don't make half as much as you guys and I swear I work harder." She ignored Ryland's snorting.

"Me, too." Hannah stood beside her sister, crossing her arms over her chest. "We can help."

Nate pushed up from his chair and approached Emma, even with the room full of all of their cousins. He knelt on the ground beside her as he looked up at her. "I don't want to leave you anymore."

"I know." She framed his face in her hands, her smile sad but tender. "I know, Nate, but now we can't worry about that."

He stared at her, as if they spoke with their gazes.

Sherri's heart took on an all new ache and she reached for Kyle's hand. They held on, watching as the entire family held their breath.

Nate was the oldest. He and Emma held them all together. What they decided, the rest of them would go along with. They always did.

Nate slowly pulled Emma's hands from his face.

Standing, he turned to take in the whole group. Emma's fingers found his and he cleared his throat. "I'll need to put the ranch up for sale."

Stefanie slumped into her seat, gasping. "You won't take money from Cyan, but you'll sell the ranch? This is my home, too. Not just yours." She bit her lip and rushed from the room.

"Nate, no." Emma grabbed his hand with both of hers, tugging as if her slight weight would budge him.

"We need to cover medical bills and what happened at the ranch. If Stefanie and Hannah are going to work with us, we'll just have to make sure we only take jobs where we can board." Nate hardened his jaw. "We'll have to figure this out."

Hannah's quiet voice broke through the shocked silence that fell around the room. "Where will Emma stay?"

Nate looked down at his wife. He gripped her shoulder and nodded hard. "It's time to call Drake."

Hard times were ahead, but at least they had each other.

And sometimes that's all that mattered.

~~~

Sherri and Kyle came through a lot of things together, but as the family faces tough times ahead, they all need to figure out a way to survive and thrive at the same time.

The end of *Unbridled Trails* book #3 of *The Montana Trails* series, Clearwater County Collection. Read *Hidden Trails*, book #4 of *The Montana Trails series* and the rest of the series. Stefanie and Drake crash together as they fight their attraction and their equal need to help family. Keep reading for a SNEAK PEEK.

Read more about Nate Rourke and Jareth Darby and their cousins, and what can make a cowboy lose his heart.

Don't forget to sign up for the Survivor newsletter for all things Paulson!

Dear Reader,

We're deep into the series with the finish of book #3. I love the stories of the Montana Trails and I promise we have many more to cover. Bear with me as we head into book 4, *Hidden Trails*, with Stephanie and Drake's story and see where Nate and Emma end up.

The family is a strong one and I know they have each other's backs, but watch for upcoming feuds and loss and love that has the potential to tear this family apart.

This book was hard for me to write from an emotional standpoint. Sherri was hard to write – let's be honest, someone who loves spiders? I mean, come on. But thanks to Team Paulson, I was able to find out that her favorite dessert is cheesecake.

Team Paulson… what would I do without you?

I'm very excited to continue with this series and I hope you are, too. I look forward to seeing you in the next book!

Don't hesitate to drop me a line and let me know what you think. Please leave a review wherever you are able. Authors need reviews more than you know!

Until the next book, if you'd like to see more of me, follow me on social media and sign up for my newsletter.

Stay Alive,

Bonnie

Unbridled Trails, book 4

Prologue

Drake

Uncle Will plopped into the plush micro-suede easy chair across from Drake's office desk. He sighed, lifting the worn sole of his black tennis shoe and resting it across his knee. "I'll never get used to the comfort in here. It's so much better than even at home." He glanced around the amply furnished office and then at Drake. "It's pretty lonely though. I brought you some mail."

Drake glanced up from a financial marketing plan he'd been perusing and studied his uncle. "Mail? You haven't gotten my mail in a couple years." He'd moved out of his uncle's home a long time ago, well not like a decade or anything, but long enough he couldn't think of anyone who wouldn't have his address.

Except the people claiming to be his parents.

He set his bone pen on the desk and folded his hands. "Is it from *them*?" He didn't need to name any names. Uncle Will knew Drake wasn't interested in the Bensons. There weren't many people Drake couldn't stand, but his parents ranked at the top of the short list.

His palms itched as his breath quickened. Why couldn't they just leave well enough alone? Why did they have to wait until he'd settled so comfortably into his life? Why couldn't they just stay out of it? They were absent so long, he'd grown adapted to the sensation of abandonment, to where it didn't hurt or bother him as much. Then they'd contact him and stir the whole messy pot of emotions.

Uncle Will extended a creamy peach envelope clutched in his fingers. "It *is* from your family. But remember when you mentioned at dinner a few nights ago that you wouldn't mind if they disappeared from this earth?" He arched his eyebrows, concern marring his otherwise stoic expression. "Son, you need to be careful what you wish for."

He didn't wish for anything. Not anymore. Not when he could buy whatever he wanted. Drake had given up longing for anything – except one thing. One person. But she was so far out of reach. He would have to deal with the family issue before he'd ever be able to wish for her.

"Did you read it? If you read it, just tell me what it says so I don't have to deal with my mother's insipid whining." Drake ignored the envelope his uncle placed carefully in front of him.

Carefully shaking his head and frowning, Uncle Will said reproachfully. "Drake, I don't read other people's mail. I just know something's off. The letter is thick and it's addressed to you – not in your mother's handwriting." He leaned forward, tapping the top of the padded rectangle with a firm finger. "And I don't mind saying, it has the scent of apricots about it."

"Apricots?" Curiosity piqued, Drake stole a glance at the envelope. Thick. Good news never came with thick mail. So many people had turned to email, getting snail mail was uncommon anymore.

Drake picked up the missive and turned it over. The slanty writing had more of a quiver to it than he remembered, but he'd recognize Emma's letter *B* anywhere.

He hadn't heard from his older sister in forever. To be fair, he hadn't encouraged communication with her after the first year. Talking with her was too painful, too drawn out.

When she'd stopped asking when he was returning, he'd stopped wondering when he would see her again.

With an ivory handled letter opener he'd gotten from his uncle at graduation, Drake slit open the top crease of the envelope. About five pictures fell onto the desk and then he pulled out a tightly folded collection of paper, maybe four or five.

"Do you mind, if I read this to myself first?" Drake didn't want to read anything out loud and be surprised. Who knew what bomb his sister had hidden in there? She wasn't known for subtlety.

Of course, he would share it with Uncle Will. Their relationship didn't have many secrets. Drake just didn't want to read it before he'd had a chance to assimilate the information.

Thankfully, his uncle loved Drake almost more than his own children. He nodded and pulled out a novel he'd rolled up and tucked into his back pocket.

"Take your time, I've been dying to see what Ole' L'Amour is going to do to this hero."

Drake,

It's back.

I'm not getting treatment.

I love you.

Emma

Like a horrible haiku, her simple words smacked of energy depletion and effort. How hard had it been for her to talk of "it" like an old friend?

She didn't have to name *it*.

It had ruled the majority of the lives for so long, *it* had almost become part of the family. Resentment jammed through him. Of course, the corrupt cancer and its stinging grasp would reach him in Wyoming.

Drake flipped through the pages she'd included of medical reports and tests and even photocopies of scans. Anger twisted his mouth. Why couldn't he escape the bitterness of her diagnoses from so far away? Why did the pain of her declaration of no treatment hurt so much? Because having her alive and accessible meant he'd have the chance to see her again. When he was ready.

Not when the cancer was ready.

Once again, Emma's disease ruled his life. Once again, the cancer claimed his freedom and stole away his choices. Shortening the time he had to adapt to the idea.

And Emma wasn't innocent. By choosing not to have treatment, she was choosing to speed things along. Choosing to give in.

Like hell. He'd go back and shake some sense into her. Drake would go back and do what needed to be done. Judging by her reports, things were progressing a lot faster than they did when they were

361

younger. He glanced up at his uncle and stood. "Looks like I'm going home."

Chapter 1

2006

Stefanie

Stefanie traced the whorls and lines of the wood grain in her father's desk with the tip of her finger. Over the span of her life the character of the wood had softened, faded with wear. She adjusted her cheek on the side of her bicep as she lay across her arm on the desk.

If she closed her eyes and breathed in slow, she could just smell her dad's favorite soap with a hint of pine. He used to push his palm to the wood and then slap out of a rhythm only he could hear. She'd loved that.

How many years had she sat there with Dad before he'd died? Even more since he'd gone? She tried so hard to stay on top of the books but money had to come in in order for it to go out.

Instead, all it did was trickle in and gush out. And there was nothing she could do to control it.

She didn't own Bella Acres.

Her brother did.

She didn't have financial control over its upkeep and bills.

Her brother did.

Nate's most pressing concern – even over the welfare of their home – was his wife's declining health.

Stefanie got it. She did. But if they weren't more careful, Emma would die in the backwoods of Clearwater County while the rest of them begged for food on the dirt roads in the small town of Taylor Falls.

She sighed, unwilling to move. Maybe they could rent out the back quarter - no that wouldn't work because access would have to go through the rest of the property which would require more fencing.

More fencing meant more money they didn't have. Sliding up from the desk, she plopped her elbow onto the edge of the desk and rested her chin in her hand, twirling the click pen she couldn't get to work right. The stupid thing would write for a little bit and then fade, then write a bit more, then fade.

They didn't even have enough money to buy properly working pens.

A soft knock on the door announced her brother, Nate. He strolled in, his smile questioning as he perused the office, probably checking for something else to sale. "I'm surprised you're in here and not packing."

Stefanie scoffed, leaning back in the seat and pushing herself side to side. "Why would I be packing? We're not supposed to go on the market for another four months. That's taking preparedness a little too far, even for you, Nate." She maintained a joking tone, but inside bitterness at her brother's cavalier attitude over the impending sale of their home ate at her like acid on leather.

Nate claimed the seat across from her. Crossing his ankle to rest on his knee, he picked at a string on his boot and avoided Stefanie's gaze. He cleared his throat. "Emma's getting worse - fast. I'm opting for voluntary auction, but the bank will only do one every quarter. That puts the next one in four weeks. Not four months." He looked up, piercing Stefanie with his eyes. "I need the money sooner rather than later,

Stef. You know I wouldn't be doing this, if it wasn't… about her."

Captiva Publishing

Bonnie R. Paulson

www.bonniepaulson.com

Printed in Great Britain
by Amazon